NIGHTTIME KINGDOM

WILLIAM J. O'BRIEN

Foreword by
T. Cole Rachel

Copyright © 2024 by William J. O'Brien

All rights reserved. No part of this publication may be reproduced, distributed, or transmitted in any form or by any means, including photocopying, recording, or other electronic or mechanical methods, without the prior written permission of the publisher, except in the case of brief quotations embodied in critical reviews and certain other noncommercial uses permitted by copyright law.

This is a work of fiction. Names, characters, places, and incidents either are the product of the author's imagination or are used fictitiously. Any resemblance to actual persons, living or dead, businesses, events, or locales is entirely coincidental.

ISBN: 979-8-9902311-0-8 (first edition hardback), 979-8-9902311-1-5 (hardback), 979-8-9902311-2-2 (paperback), 979-8-9902311-3-9 (epub), 979-8-9902311-4-6 (paperback), 979-8-9902311-5-3 (epub)

Published by Shadow Work Press

Foreword by: T. Cole Rachel

Cover design by Ben Tousley

Drawings by William J. O'Brien

Printed in United States

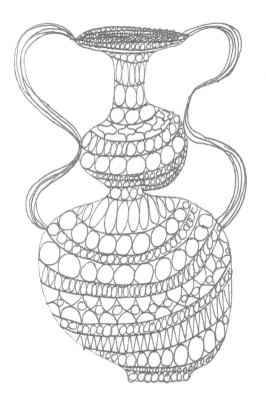

*Dedicated to my tender
& beloved Ed*

"After the drama, he had to live in the tragedy."

—Jean Genet

Author's Note

In the fall of 2012, I suffered a studio fire where I completely lost everything. Many years later, I wanted to write a book that addressed how we process and deal with loss, grief, and trauma. Ted, the main character in *Nighttime Kingdom,* is an emotional characterization of that period based around the tragic events of the Apple Butter Festival of 1983 in Hubert, Ohio.

We are in a very difficult time where many of us feel powerless and are losing hope regarding both the state of the world and the increasing polarity of those who have power, and those who feel powerless. Although this is a fictional story, it is my hope that this book offers a transparent lens into the importance of queer intimacy, the value of our relationships, and moreover, how anyone who has experienced challenging circumstances that feel powerless can find hope and meaning.

There is no right or wrong way to heal. There is no right or wrong way to fall in love. There is no right or wrong way to deal with tragedy or loss. During the winter of 2023, I channeled and wrote this story. I kept having dreams and visions and approached writing this story the same way that I approach making my artwork. My intention was to embody and channel

Author's Note

the wounds, love, and messiness into a story that presented the complications of anyone on the path towards healing.

Everyone has a right to be creative, deserves an audience, and deserves space to be seen and respected. Unfortunately, many times as artists, we do not feel this way. We are constantly given feedback, direction, and unsolicited guidance on what we should do with our work. In the end, artists make the final decision. Everyone deserves to be seen. Everyone deserves to be heard. Everyone has a right to express their voice and story.

This is my story. My hope is that it will allow the reader to touch in with their own tenderness, to feel the world completely, to be in touch with one's heart.

— William J. O'Brien

Trigger Warning: This book delves into sensitive themes, portraying scenes of emotional distress and the aftermath of past trauma. Reader discretion is advised, as individuals who may be triggered by these topics are encouraged to approach the material with caution. Resources for support and guidance are available at the end of the book, including helplines, crisis intervention services, and organizations specializing in mental health and trauma recovery.

Foreword
By T. Cole Rachel

Feeling it.

I was recently asked what was the first 'gay' novel I ever remember reading and I felt embarrassed that I could not immediately answer. Despite growing up without the internet to help me, I was a precocious teen reader and explorer of libraries, having no trouble searching out gay and queer-coded literature to devour in secret. And while it was both thrilling and vaguely comforting to read books by Edmund White, John Rechy, and James Baldwin, given my own very limited experiences (I never met another out gay person until the age of 19, after I went to college) these books often felt as if they were written in a foreign language, beamed in from a distant planet that I myself would likely never visit. It wasn't until the '90s, reading books like Scott Heim's *Mysterious Skin* or Jim Grimsley's *Dream Boy*, that I encountered something that felt as if it were taking place in the same world that I actually lived in. There is nothing quite as shocking or revelatory as having your own experience reflected back at you in a piece of art and it was a jolt I felt over and over again while reading William J.

Foreword

O'Brien's *Nighttime Kingdom.* So much about the book was instantly familiar, not only in its depiction of what it means to flee your small town and head to the big city (a tale as old as time, especially for so many gay people), but also in it's descriptions of the ways in which love and intimacy remain our most valuable (and frequently elusive) human currencies.

There is a moment about midway through the novel in which the protagonist, experiencing the full emotional landslide of falling in love for the first time as a closeted teenager, must suddenly reckon with what it really means to see an abstract desire made real. While first experiencing what it means to love and be loved, he must also learn to negotiate the realities of queer affection in a world where such things are still verboten: "It is a strange feeling to long for someone but to also suffer in silence," he thinks. "To feel a sense of desire and craving that is quelled by the fear of discovery. You walk around, remaining behind others in power who parade their lives in front of yours and are unaware of the privilege they wield. You suffer in silence behind them. It is learned by watching. When to lock eyes. When to avoid contact. When to move."

It's but one of many moments that stopped me in my tracks while reading O'Brien's haunting book, which not only unpacks the inherent complications of coming of age as a queer person, but examines the ways in which that experience is all too often part and parcel with some form of abject trauma. As a person who came of age in a small town in middle America back in the relatively dark ages of the 1980s, the emotional wallop of *Nighttime Kingdom* was akin to experiencing pain from a phantom limb that I had forgotten was once attached to my body. I cannot fully imagine what it must be like to be a young gay person today, buoyed, one would hope, by access to the internet, cultural visibility, and a variety of resources, but I

Foreword

suspect that in the deep pockets of middle America, the experience is often largely the same. So much of my own experience as a young gay person was characterized by fear and a kind of hypervigilant awareness of how I presented (careful never to say the wrong thing, reveal myself too much in mixed company) and exerting extreme caution regarding my surroundings (never staying late alone at school, walking home late, or going to any event where no adults were present) as to avoid making myself feel even more vulnerable. It was, as I experienced it, both harrowing and exhausting — the kind of emotional high wire act that O'Brien's book captures perfectly. These experiences stay with us, and generally color the way we move through the world for the rest of our lives.

Nighttime Kingdom is many things — a coming of age tale, a document of loss, a treatise on the lifelong imprints of trauma, a love story — but in the end it's much more than that. "There are minor losses. And losses that are life changing." O'Brien writes, "Both are similar in the reactions they trigger in the spirit, heart, and soul. Then there are those losses which reverberate so deeply that they forever reshape the fundamental structure of who we are." The characters in *Nighttime Kingdom* remind us that even though tragedy can break us, it can also be transformative in ways we don't expect — it can be the jet fuel that propels us into a different (hopefully better) kind of life, it can be the catalyst for making us stronger and (again, hopefully) more empathetic, more fully realized, and truly loving creatures. Though I wish it were not the case, sometimes you have to feel all the bad in order to feel any of the good. This book reminded me of why it's worth it.

— T. Cole Rachel

Chapter 1
Hand to Cheek

Slaps can be disciplinary—forcing a child to learn from their behavior—and then there are the more philosophical slaps. The deeper slaps. The slaps symbolizing a more important lesson that should be felt from the hand of the giver to the cheek of the receiver.

It had been several weeks since Ted Krieger had buried his father, Ted Sr., when he found himself sitting in his therapist's office and discussing topics including, but not limited to, his childhood and what had brought him into therapy in the first place.

"I recognize that it is difficult for you to call to mind any good memories of your father, but I think it would be helpful, in trying to process this grief, to ruminate and recall good memories you had with him," Dr. Kathryn stated.

"I agree, and I am trying, but I am also still contemplating my fear of the reality that someone can still hurt you from the grave."

As the light slowly faded in the room, Ted shifted his gaze

to the arrangement of small, intimately curated plants on the shelf to the left of Kathryn, and then to the view out the window of a park overlooking Fifth Avenue. The plants each had a distinct characteristic to them, as if they were a group of angels singing in harmony as the sun danced and played off the windowsill.

"In the end, I know there will be no total resolution here, I am just striving towards placing all of this somewhere that gives me some space to move forward without feeling like I am constantly looking over my shoulder."

"That's fair. It takes time, Ted."

The light in the room that afternoon in session reminded him of the turn of the fall season back in his hometown of Hubert, Ohio. Fall there was always one of the most important times of year. It was *the* season—some would say more important than the holidays—as it symbolized the end of summer, the beginning of harvest season, and the infamous Hubert Apple Butter Festival. It marked the beginning of a new school year.

The wallpaper in Dr. Kathryn's office reminded him of a similar seventies motif from the ground floor bathroom of his childhood home. That arrangement of rectangles, angular lines, and highlights of silver and grey somewhat resembled a symbol of a pineapple. Ted always wondered who made these choices for wallpaper. Some interior designer somewhere must have somehow thought it conducive to making people feel either safe enough to talk about the traumas of their past or go to the bathroom in peace, he mused, or perhaps they were just really into pineapples. They were probably one of those pathological people who put pineapple on pizza! This type of cynicism always accompanied Ted when contending with his past and the strong emotions it stirred up. It was an easy and quick coping mechanism. Would it not be easier to make a joke or

Nighttime Kingdom

brush off this pain instead of admitting its cause or source? But he knew he had to try. Or at least fake an effort towards resolution. In many ways the question of definition, or an ending, or beginning of where time and memories exist always plagued Ted. Ever since birth, he'd felt his life was playing out in reverse.

"Doc... is it essential to return to the beginning, that is the past, to find resolution in the present? Does that not sound like a loaded cliché?"

It felt hard to reconcile that sentiment with all the advice he offered his own clients, as a career counselor, including platitudes such as, "Sometimes you do not know what you are meant to be, where you are meant to go, or what you want to do. The best course of direction is to say to yourself, okay, I know I do not want this, or that, or to be affiliated with this particular direction, and then that sets you on a different route that at least sounds truer to your core values of what is important."

Dr. Kathryn was silent for a moment before concluding the session by saying, "The path towards healing is never linear. I recommend you allow yourself the grace to find, as you stated, the right direction perhaps by not knowing where to go but by allowing yourself the grace to be surprised by what you may find along the way."

All this conversation about the past, and everything related to his point of origin always left Ted emotionally exhausted. Being a surface dweller had always appeased him. Just numbing out. Compartmentalizing. Blowing everything off as no big deal. But he knew that was not the answer, and that it was what had brought him back into therapy in the first place.

His return to therapy was precipitated by experiencing stronger emotional reactions to mundane events, and his coping mechanisms growing increasingly unskillful. There'd been a spell of uncontrollable crying for hours after the produce clerk told him, "Sorry we are just out of plums this season, you will just have to substitute a different stone fruit for your tart." And he'd broken down, screaming in anger, after a teenager decided to take his seat at the local coffee house or on the subway, "It is your inconsideration! That is why this city is, and will always be, a terrible place to live." Usual mid-life crisis type-of-deal, right? But, as everyone knows, once you land back in the chair it inevitably leads back to the beginning, those first relationships, brittle bonding, raw experiences, mommy and daddy issues, etc.

The fresh air on Fifth Avenue felt so much better as he started walking back to his office. It was September in New York City, which was always a nice time to be there. Families were returning to the city from their summer trips, and extended stays on Long Island or Upstate. Everyone was going back to school. It always felt like a fresh start. A turning over of new leaves. New clothes. New me. New start.

When walking down 24th Street, he always enjoyed stopping by Madison Square Park. Even if just to criss cross over to Park Avenue South, get a small coffee from a street vendor, and then slowly return to the office, it afforded him an opportunity to compartmentalize and return to a sense of normality and some semblance of routine. As he sat down on his favorite bench that allowed him a view of the Flatiron Building, where he'd first worked as an assistant upon arriving in the city almost twenty years ago, he saw it was now being converted into condos. Was anything left sacred in this city anymore? Dr. Kathryn was right. He was avoiding feeling and giving himself grace about the past, but his current life in New York was so different from the life he began in Hubert. He'd spent most of his adult life trying to forget the events of the summer/early fall

Nighttime Kingdom

of 1983. Sitting on the green bench, he was watching a young boy, of perhaps nine or ten, and his mother sitting across from him on another bench and sharing a croissant in peace, enjoying the view of bicycles, fast walkers, and throngs of people eating their lunches quickly in-between the next thing to do. All of them were snatching moments of peace before the next storm to be weathered. It reminded him of the few and far between memories he held of his mother, Rita Krieger, back before she'd left town when he was around the same age as the boy.

The earliest memories he had of Rita were generally pleasant, if undeniably tinged with some edginess. But her absence had been so long, and having not been in contact ever since made those memories take on a mirage-like quality; dreams, mere shells of what was before. It had become apparent that before and after, but also at this point, the importance of him letting go of any expectations was paramount. Though he had contacted her once recently, back when he was about to get married to his partner, Sam, who had been very insistent on contacting her despite Ted's ambivalence. He'd made several attempts. At that point, she was living in a hippie community somewhere outside of Taos, without a telephone or mailing address. Unreachable. Did it make sense to try to reach out to her and tell her about Ted Sr.'s passing? Was it important or relevant at this point?

Just as he was about to get up, he saw his close friend Felix walking towards him to sit down. Felix had just returned from the city, after a wonderful summer in Sant Marten working at a high-end resort in Anse Marcel.

"Well, hello hello! Nice to see you Felix," said Ted, giving him a close hug, "How was your summer?"

"It was good, so nice to leave the city, but as you know, there is no escape. We blame the city for all our problems, only to be humbled when they follow us. Happy to be back though. How are you?"

"Good, good, ya know... the usual wrestling of existential crises consumes me, but the everyday is manageable. Trying to figure out what I'm doing with myself. So, yeah, the usual. Let's get together soon with Sam for drinks. Maybe we can go to the Phoenix, like the old days?" "Yes let's do that. Be well, I'll text you next week."

Felix responded quickly, "Sorry I forgot about tonight. Duh, I will see you later at Shantel's engagement party. Am still on island time here!"

"No worries! See you later!"

They both hugged and kissed, and Felix strode off.

Felix Morgan was first friends with Sam Klein, Ted's current partner, and had been since their NYU days. But everyone had met up around the same time in the city. Ted always was enamored with Felix's subtle taste and style that came from his upbringing in Massachusetts and having attended boarding schools. The old money he came from was as substantial as it was subtle, disguised or hidden based on his demeanor and appearance. There were only flickering hints of his blue blood Anglo heritage, such as his most recent casual trip to the Caribbean, or the fact he somehow lived very well in NYC while only working part-time as a yoga instructor. Of course, there was also his refined taste in fashion that ran the gamut from subtle athleisure wear, to strategic items he'd play off as lucky vintage thrift finds if questioned, but which were clearly heirlooms from his grandfather's haute couture leftovers. Ted felt relieved that Sam and Ted had such an unshakeable friendship. They'd met over twenty years ago, at Steinhardt, which in Ted's observation was the Montessori version of higher education. It felt as if the curriculum was based on personal preference and changed on a dime, from focusing on the intersections of performance art one day, to incorporating and training to become an acoustic musician the next. Felix always reminded him of his sister, Janelle Krieger, a free spirit who at times seemed clueless but possessed an unquestionably good heart and was a good person.

Felix and Sam were once lovers, though that was long ago. Their friendship had since evolved, as most metro-non-hetero relationships do, into a harmony of the personal, political, and sexual. It was the perfect manifestation of chosen family and Ted, frankly, was relieved by the changed dynamic. Although he truly loved Sam, the man had a lot of energy to express and consistently needed to be in the midst of an active social sphere. Ted preferred extended periods of silence and quiet contemplation. While living in the city, such times could only be found sitting in deconsecrated churches, those little single-occupant unisex bathrooms at bookstores, on long walks through leafy neighborhoods with headphones on, sitting on park benches, or riding the train aimlessly for hours. Choosing which escape for Ted was always a struggle, as was determining when and how it was appropriate to drink alone.

As Ted watched Felix walk off, he was reminded of the party later that day and of last night's uncomfortable conversation with Sam. It hadn't been a new one. It was a conversation they'd had many times around Sam feeling that Ted was not present, emotionally, or to be frank not present at all with him when they were together. Sam snapping his fingers in front of a glassy-eyed Ted was a common occurrence, saying, "Hello, I am here, where are you?" and for Ted once again to feel ashamed since he was not intentionally drifting off. He just found remaining tethered to the moment and not drifting off into his own head so hard. It was common to for him to wake to someone asking him a question or, in the case with Sam, feeling genuinely ignored.

Ted got off the bench with a sigh and started walking towards his office that was in the Metropolitan North Building. Ever since moving to NYC, he'd loved and admired the history of all the buildings. He felt a special pride that his office was inside. Officially a New Yorker. Every day represented a new adventure with a sense of magic coursing through the beautiful loggias that guarded the entrance. But today he could not go back in. He knew that he'd been triggered in his session with Dr. Kathryn, and so decided to keep walking towards his favorite neighborhood store on Lexington that carried the most impressive array of spices and a lovely deli that he would occasionally get mujaddara sandwiches from to bring back to the office. Despite the frustration of seeing most of his clients only on video, connecting to the neighborhood businesses that had been neglected since the pandemic was something he enjoyed. Though the hybrid model wasn't all bad, since it came with the undeniable benefit of none of his bosses working on site and so his prolonged absences such as this one oftentimes went unnoticed. Stepping inside the store, he was struck by the smell of all the spices. The aisles and bags were all lined up with different colors contained in plastic packages waiting to be used and expressed like little kids waiting to be picked for kickball. It flung his mind back to gym class at Hubert Public School. There were always the more popular spices like turmeric, nutmeg, cumin, and fennel seeds arranged next to those less popular, like pumpkin spice mix, or Italian herb medley. Ted always wondered who would buy such generic blends at a specialty store such as this, since the whole point of coming here was surely to get the best product, most likely for a specialized recipe. Spices had been an integral part of his upbringing in Hubert, Ohio. They were the lifeblood and sustenance for the town. You could say they were more valuable than anything else. The right spices determined the best product. Apples, applesauce, apple juice, cider, apple donuts... anything that could possibly be made out of apples was made in that place. It was strange to consider how most people affiliated these spices with comfort or home, with morning oatmeal, the occasional pumpkin pie, or apple fritters. For Ted, it was a complex range of body memories they provoked. He naturally gravitated towards the cinnamon, picked up a small bag and drew it close to his nose before inhaling. Grandma Krieger would always pull Ted aside in the kitchen to talk about the healing nature of spices. How could something so pure as the scent of cinnamon bring back such bitterness and sadness in him?

It was unavoidable. He felt the tell-tale warmth in his hands. Then the shaking of his fingertips. Then it rode through his chest. Soon enough, his face became flushed. His heart raced and chest tightened and breath started tumbling in ragged bursts and everything somehow spun in all directions at once and he darted outside and vomited into the metal garbage can at the intersection of Lexington and 28th.

Chapter 2
Town of Hubert, Ohio

The town of Hubert, Ohio is a typical Midwestern town. Initially settled as a colony in the late seventeen hundreds as a stopping point for pioneers traveling west in search of their fortunes in silver and gold, once Erie Canal was established it became a frequent stop for trade, and subsequently became known for its agricultural potential. Apples were always entwined with the history and heart of Hubert. It was widely known that every townsperson knew just as much, if not more, about apples than most people would about sports cars, or any other such standard Americana interests.

If you took a map of Lake Erie, divided it in half, and drew a dotted line from north to south you would find Hubert smack dab in the middle. It's nested precisely in-between Cleveland and Meadville. The town was strategically located near the Ohio Valley as the weather systems just south of the lake favored a good meteorological combination to water and harvest the apple orchards for most of the season. Hubert was officially named and founded by Raymond Hillcrest in 1795. Hillcrest had emigrated with his family from Germany, specifically the Rhineland region, and was determined to claim the fortunes of the New World by applying his family history of farming. The Hillcrest family knew apples; how to plant, farm, harvest, and profit from them.

No one can say for sure who planted the first apple tree in Hubert, and there are many conflicting stories from three different sources. The earliest of these is from the Native American Lenni Lenape tribe, who frequently passed through the Ohio Valley in alignment with the seasons and would plant, and then on their return, harvest different crops which included apples that were naturally present from the beginning. The second story, supported by many generations of townsfolk, was that Johnny Appleseed was responsible for planting the first apple trees in Hubert. The last, and longest standing tale, tells of Raymond Hillcrest planting seeds he'd sewn into his jacket across the Atlantic Ocean as they were one of the most precious items to bring into the New World. Until just a few years ago, Hillcrest Orchards owned and operated most all of the apple orchards, with the exception of a few specialized farms, that have endured since the time of the earliest settlers.

When Greg Hillcrest was the CEO of Hillcrest, Inc. and was the same age as Ted Krieger Sr, he married a woman named Helen. They had only one child, Jerome Krieger, who was the same age as Ted. Over the years, the Hillcrest orchards grew at the same rate as the town, and still employs most of the citizens of Hubert at either the cannery, retail store, corporate headquarters, or in the fields. Hillcrest Farms are probably most known currently as the mainstay of Hubert. They produce most of the crop of apples for the entire Midwest region, and oftentimes cause her to draw comparisons with Northern Michigan, except instead of cherries it is apples.

For as long as Ted could remember, and galvanized by

stories told by his grandparents, the Krieger family had always worked for Hillcrest Orchards (with the only exception being Ted's great grandfather, George Krieger, who took a different route and was the mailman for the town of Hubert). Apples and the success of apples was the backbone of Hubert's economy. During the entire planting, growing, and harvesting season, everyone in the town was acutely aware of weather patterns, temperature, soil conditions, and all the variables that could affect a good harvest. If there was a good harvest that year, it meant the town was financially viable, while a bad harvest meant people would struggle for the next year.

In the center of Hubert stands an oval town square, with a

park and a log cabin in the center. That log cabin was the first structure erected in the town but has since come to serve as the Hubert Center for Tourism. Inside the log cabin stand several retail displays depicting the timelines of the history of the town, as well as the production of her apple products. There are displays of the various antique instruments that were used over the generations to harvest apples, make cider, and churn apple butter, Additionally, the store carries all manner of products derived from apples: strudels, taffy apples, apple candy, apple candles, lotion, shampoos, along with anything which can be made or enhanced by apples that you could possibly imagine. And then some more.

Encircling the town square are historical houses and businesses, many having endured since their first creation at the turn of the century. It is considered a mark of pride to have a special century plaque on the outside of your home designating it as one of the original structures of when the town was built. To the right of the square, on the south side, is the Hubert Village Inn and Restaurant that serves as a frequent stop for tour buses that roll through mainly in the picturesque fall, when the leaves turn, and the Apple Butter Festival is held when mostly all of them have browned, in September. The restaurant serves historical colonial dishes that highlight the history of Hubert and the employees don colonial period outfits. At one point, Ted and his sister Janelle worked there. Ted was fired for breaking a stack of dishes as a busboy and was frankly relieved by it since every time he did something wrong as a line cook the head chef would strike his hands.

To the right of the town square is Hubert Public Library and School, which was originally the town hall but became primarily used for the different groups and clubs to meet. It was also used as both the grade school and high school, while still housing civic offices for the city. The blue building retains the

Nighttime Kingdom

remnants of Victorian design and is ringed by the intricate carving of both a white picket fence and the trusses inside that bare a wooden engraved sign of two hands clasped, holding an apple. Above the door there still hangs an original wood panel that reads: "Hubert, Ohio, established, 1795" under which an additional engraved wooden plaque bears the town's motto:

> "To sacrifice oneself for the sake of another is the ultimate service to community and should be paired and met with ease with the expectations of mothers, fathers, sons and daughters."

The building had multiple uses over the years, and as such came to be considered the main artery of Hubert by hosting community gatherings and any important town events. Ted Krieger Sr. was one of the presidents of the employee union which frequently held its monthly meetings regarding any ongoing issues with the Hillcrest Corporation there. These agendas included things such as employee issues, adequate compensation, insurance, and intellectual property rights concerning new recipes used within the cannery.

The Krieger home sits just off town square, at 43 Middleton Road. It was originally the Hubert horse storage barn and was erected around the same time as the town was founded, though for the past 75 years its function was housing the Krieger family. Ted's great grandfather, George, stumbled upon it during one of his mail routes and upon getting engaged to Roberta Krieger, made a down payment before proceeding to remodel it into a habitable dwelling. The house presently has few traces of its previous life as a stable, except on rare occasions. When Ted was a child, he would find the odd horseshoe in the basement behind a wood beam, or even a scrap of paper detailing the cost for upkeep of one of the horses that was owned by the Hillcrest family for recreation and equestrian competitions. Ted's childhood room was one of the last remaining relics of its previous life as a horse storage barn, since it bore the precise dimensions of the last remaining stall. The paneling on the walls is of different types of wood that communicate the time markers of the transition. Containing a total of four bedrooms, with three downstairs consisting of Grandma Krieger's room until her passing, as well as Janelle and Ted's, the bedrooms all met off the kitchen/living room area. A sliding glass door to the back of the kitchen leads to a small deck area that looks out on the apple orchards and offers a view of sunrise and sunset. A couple of crawl spaces are throughout the home, with some being used as storage and one off Ted's room he used as a hidden crawl space cove.

The Hillcrest estate is located just at the end of Middleton Road, past the Krieger home, as the last house at the end of a cul-de-sac with the Hillcrest Orchards spanning out behind it. To the left of the Hillcrest manor is Hillcrest Cannery and Corporate Headquarters. The Hillcrest Orchards occupies almost 120 acres total, and consists of a wide variety of 38 different types of apples. The Hillcrest Corporation's namesake and legacy is inexorably tied to their applesauce recipes. Once a year, a specially released edition of apple cider and apple butter is released by them to coincide with the annual Hubert Apple Butter Festival.

Chapter 3
Daddy Issues

What a strange phenomenon it is to grow up desiring invisibility and to have the world see only one side of who you really are.

"What a mess! Get it together, Junior," he thought to himself, echoing the voice of his late father, Ted Sr. He exhaled hard and sat down outside the spice store, on the steps of the closest stoop, then took out a handkerchief. Looking down, he wiped speckles of his breakfast from his shoes. It was always humbling to have to contend with the ghosts of the past creeping in when he needed to be a functional adult. There was no time for this nonsense, especially with Sam and him slated to host Shantel's engagement party later that day.

"Get it together, Ted Krieger, Jr," he muttered.

He gazed at the rabble of eager commuters passing by and noticed the shapes of their shoes meet up with the lines of their bodies as their shadows then intercepted contours of the buildings. The sidewalk was riddled with stains, either from the weather or some mishap the night before. Today's stain would be from Ted. The quick steps of the pedestrians were amplified as he tried to catch his breath by focusing on a small mirror that was placed inside a building and facing out towards the street. He was at once enamored with and terrified of this type of peculiar urban moment that showcased the mystifying edges of the city. There was no functional use for this mirror, unless intended for some type of urban satanic ritual. It faced outwards from the first-floor window of this nondescript bedroom. He hovered, then swayed in front of the mirror to fix his hair. Feeling disgusted with himself, and the ghosts of the past, he paused to watch the heaves and sighs of energy of the commuters and listen to their steps and feel the wind on his cheeks.

What happened was really what it was. The plights of city living. Residue from a rough night. Broken bags of trash that came undone. The singular gloves and discarded headbands that'd accumulated greasy grime. All of these were lost arti-facts of urban dwellers. The walkers quickly meandered around it all, including the fresh addition of the dregs of Ted's breakfast that didn't quite make it into the garbage can. It was just another small obstacle on an otherwise uneventful Tuesday for them. If the sun came out that day, it might dry it up and bake a pavement pizza. Eventually, it would become unrecognizable amidst the other historical stains on the concrete sidewalk.

Acute self-consciousness in the wake of falling apart was usual for Ted. He'd spent his whole childhood hiding, guard-ing, containing the wounds and events of his past. It somehow manifested in the small cracks and edges that seeped out around the edges, revealing what was underneath. As Grandma Krieger always used to say, "It takes only a small scratch to reveal the wounds of the past within someone's heart." Well, today those wounds had been torn open and

Nighttime Kingdom

oozed out in the most disgusting way at the intersection of Lex and 28th.

Ted gradually got back on his feet and started walking south, down Lexington Avenue towards Union Square. He passed by Gramercy Park on his left and glanced through the gates, transporting his mind back to the Hillcrest Family Garden back in Hubert, Ohio. It was probably built around the same time, and intended for a singular purpose: to keep certain people in and others out. So much about the town of Hubert was about playing the roles you were born into, without any change or discussion. If you were born into a rich family, you played that part. If you were born into a poor family, you also played that part. Hubert could not accommodate any variation from the social norms that defined its livelihood. Sons acted in such a way. Fathers acted in another. If you were a corporate type, you went to this party. If you were a factory or an orchard worker, you did not. You knew your place. However, this had changed over the past few decades thanks to the work of Ted Krieger Sr.'s union organizing. There'd been a shift to make the town more accessible. It extended the benefits of the park to all employees of Hillcrest so that any member of the public could peruse and enjoy the rare plant species that the previous generations of Hillcrests had brought back from their exotic travels around the world. In this way, redeeming qualities were not absent from Ted Sr. He was a team player. Generally liked around the town. Ted knew the private sides of Ted Sr. were a bit different. A dark spirit of sorts lurked beneath. Ted Sr. was a surface dweller.

A woman in her twenties, dressed in a fur coat, stepped out of a 1980s Red Porsche 911. The door was held open by an older man in his sixties, wearing jeans and a beige looking suede jacket clearly curated and selected by his younger lover. Such a scene is commonplace in NYC when Wall Street money meets the struggles of twenty-somethings hustling to not eat another slice of pizza for every meal. Careers have been built on such trysts, and some even land the ultimate meal ticket to a rarefied existence in the suburbs of Connecticut. The man postured on the sidewalk, preventing Ted from walking past so his young belle could gracefully walk into the restaurant across from Gramercy Park for an overpriced lunch. Ted sighed and muttered to himself, "God, what is with straight douchebags with small dicks and sports cars?"

"You say something, pal?" the guy cut back.

Ted replied, "No, I'm good," in a tone reminiscent of his father's that'd been all too familiar to him growing up.

The interaction brought him back to Hubert, Ohio. Since Ted's mom, Rita, left when he was nine, Ted Sr. had become obsessed with two main things: sports cars and women. The former only ever had two seats, and the latter was occupied by a steady succession of fresh-faced blondes. That meant taking care of his children at the time couldn't even have taken a back-seat in his world. His first and all-consuming love was his sports car. That Black Ford Mustang. OMG! With those ridiculous embroidered seats! Oh, Lord! That Godforsaken sports car. He had saved up his money during his old football days at Hubert High School from working nights and weekends at the apple cannery to snag that thing. It had meticulously waxed glossy black paint, and red seats that Ted Sr. had personally stitched and detailed for him and Rita when they started dating. On the driver's seat, embroidered in white stitching, *King*, the passenger seat, *Queen*. You can guess how awkward it was for Ted to ride in the *Queen* passenger seat after his mom left. The irony wasn't lost on him. He sure was a *Queen* these days, but at the time such a word would not have accurately described that awkward thirteen-year-old gay kid. Ted cringed on so many levels every time he had to get into that car with his

Nighttime Kingdom

father. It bore such a distinct, desperate aroma of leather, cologne, and stale coffee. The basic trifecta of smells most desperate, single, straight men who are deeply insecure in their identities—and most probably penis sizes—reek of. Sitting in the *Queen* passenger seat on all levels represented what he wasn't, would never be, and would never live up to as a man from the Midwest. Once, on a drive back to the airport during a brief holiday season, Ted Sr. leaned back from the leather steering wheel and asked, "So, what is with this whole gay thing?" in a tone not unlike a mafia don driving to his next hit or deal. For Ted, such an exchange was their usual base line. Ted Sr. was a man of few words, preferring to communicate in grunts and physical exchanges. Bro this. Bro that. His communication was vapid and devoid of any of the emotional depth his son craved after Grandma Krieger died and his mother left unannounced.

On some level, Ted got Ted Sr. He understood his evolution and expectations and the constraints he was up against. The shackles that he had to contend with in his current reality. It was not at all what he'd expected, after having been the all-star MVP football high school running back of 1963 and earning himself a guaranteed scholarship to a Division 1 school. It was his one and only ticket out of Hubert. Ted and his sister Janelle represented a life that he inherited, but had not chosen. Like heartburn after a satisfying meal. Even when Rita got pregnant with their first child, Janelle, it was not expected. Maybe they should not have kept that baby. Ted and Janelle discussed this later, as adults, concluding that Ted Sr. was just too cheap to get an abortion. So it was that they all ended up in that horse barn together on Middleton Street, as a family. Just staring each other down. Just waiting around to die. Or get drunk.

This tension behind Ted's desire and parental neglect both

confused and plagued him. On one level, he was aware of his daddy issues and how they determined the guys he usually gravitated towards for sex before he met Sam.... those guys who were masculine, straight-presenting, and with a bitter taste of emotional unavailability. This led to many hours of conversations with Shantel about why they didn't text or call after their first hookups, eventually ending always the same way and leaving Ted feeling inadequate. Unwanted. It was the same feeling Ted Sr. left him frequently feeling as his son. There was always this subtle dance that Ted played out in his intimate relationships with men, even from the beginning. It was a desire to be taken care of that was usually mixed in with his own sexual attraction to masculine, daddy, bearish types. This was a very confusing line to negotiate between nurturing and sexual attraction.

Some people are just not meant to be mothers, or fathers, or parents. It just happens after a night of sloppy drinking and sloppier choices. From there, the decision must be made whether they will stay together for this new life that was created by accident, or get rid of it and go their separate ways. When the decision to keep a child is made—and one person clearly does not want it—everyone around that person has to contend with their misery and discontent. What was the right or wrong thing to do? It is also equally painful for that person who is the actual mother or father to see for themselves that their staying will only create more harm for themselves and the child.

Ted couldn't blame his mom for leaving. He saw how much she was suffering in trying to play contradictory roles in the small-town Hubert theater set as wife and mother. If anything, Ted can see himself in his mother. She was put in an impossible situation, torn between choosing to be who she really was versus trying to marry and stay within another person's—as well

Nighttime Kingdom

as society's—expectations of her. This was not always this case. Sometimes people do not know who they are or what they want until it is right in front of them. And then they spend years avoiding admitting to themselves who they really are deep inside. That diamond wants to come out, but it cannot. And so they live in fear of leaving, of doing what they really should do, all the while watching the diamond on their ring finger fade and pale in comparison to the one inside them.

Ted Sr. and Rita were destined to be together since Ted Sr. picked her up in his black Mustang the night of their junior prom. Could you blame her? Ted Sr. was the top running back in the state, and predestined for greatness. He was handsome, but was so much more than merely attractive. He came from a good local family, and represented a worldly knowledge that Rita had no idea existed outside of Hubert. Ted Sr. always referred to her as his *Queen*. Rita was not used to garnering so much attention and chivalry from anyone around her. Until that point in her life, she'd grown accustomed to only being offered the minimum. So, in some ways, you could say her bar was set low as far as standards were concerned. It was not that Rita was unattractive, or even average, and she had her own friends, but Ted represented the best potential future for her. And it would be outside of Hubert. He was a way out.

It was decided that they would both move out of Hubert when he was offered the athletic scholarship during senior year. The embroidery adorning his Camaro's seats of *King* and *Queen* had begun as a joke but was becoming a reality. Rita wanted to feel like a *Queen,* and Ted was her *King*. He was going to lead her to better kingdoms that were far removed from humdrum Hubert.

As you might have guessed by now, things did not exactly pan out. The month after graduation, Grandpa Krieger died in a tragic accident at Hillcrest Cannery. It'd apparently involved falling into a hot vat of boiling apple cider, but no one, especially Grandma Krieger, had the stomach to see and know the details. The only thing that was obvious was that Ted's dreams were going to be put on hold. Grandma Krieger broke the news to him while staring off into space, sitting at the kitchen, "Teddy honey I am so proud of you and the work you did to get this scholarship, but I just can't see how I am going to make ends meet here and need you to stay in Hubert for one semester till I get myself back together." How could he say no? The very next day he started working in the cannery full time. One semester soon became two, and when Rita found out she was unexpectedly pregnant with Janelle it was pretty much decided that they were staying in Hubert for the near future. So much for happily ever after! It was not as if the young couple were not still interested in leaving Hubert, but a child arriving tends to change things both drastically and forever.

After Ted was born, his mother decided she wanted to go back to community college. Ted. Sr thought it was a great idea for them to make more money. Rita said she would start taking bookkeeping and accounting classes at night and on weekends, and that it would not interfere with the obligations of being a housewife. Ted Sr. would still be the all-star, *King* of his castle, and she would still be his co-pilot. The *Queen* to his *King*. As it turned out, Rita loved school. It offered her the space to claim her own ideas and voice. It also represented autonomy and the potential for a path that was never extended to her given her previous social position in Hubert.

For the first several years of Ted's life, one could say they had the most normal existence anyone could hope for as a nuclear family. Everyone was content doing what sons and daughters and mothers and fathers are supposed to do. Tensions started to mount after Rita took her first political science class. Her professor at the time, Dr. Miller, was a

Vietnam vet activist turned teacher but still had the edginess Rita had so adored in Ted Sr. back in the day, on the football field. He was confident. A risk-taker. An adventurer. Worldly. Cosmopolitan.

It started out with Rita wanting to go to a political conference one weekend in Pittsburgh. She did so. Then, slowly but surely, she began spending more and more time away from the family. It only really started to be an issue for Ted Sr. when, instead of there being a fresh hot meal on the table after his shift, there was a frozen casserole with a note tell telling—not asking—when she was to return. A *King* does not eat frozen food. Where is my *Queen?* As time went on, the fighting started. Then it got worse. Janelle would take Ted to her bedroom and they would listen to the pop albums on loan from the Hubert Public Library to drown out the noise of dishes breaking and doors being slammed. A background soundtrack to a failed marriage and dreams.

The morning that Rita left, she packed Janelle and Ted a very fresh, wonderful lunch and left a note inside for both of them, "Just know you are my greatest treasures and I will always love you." From that day on, Rita was gone. Ted Sr. was in total denial at first. He was waiting and waiting and then, when it started to dawn on him she was never coming back, the drinking took her place. Thankfully, Grandma Krieger was still alive to fill in the blanks. At least for a time. The stress of everything eventually proved too much though, and she passed away just two years after Rita left.

When the summer of 1983 rolled around, Janelle and Ted were well versed latchkey kids. They had to be, since Ted Sr. was simply not capable. Janelle and Ted bonded a great deal during that period. They both developed remarkable culinary prowess and could masterfully produce mouthwatering grilled cheese, as well as apple turnovers made by coring apples and then filling them with brown sugar, cinnamon, and nutmeg. And, of course, they were schooled in the greatest hits and variations on macaroni and cheese by either adding tuna, ground beef, or whatever else was around that Ted Sr managed to bring home.

The emotionally distant seed between Ted and his father was planted and grew during those years leading up the summer of 1983. His father would either be hungover or drunk, sitting in the kitchen with his pants half unbuckled, drinking beer after beer and then stumbling eventually into his own abyss. He would stop and just stare at Ted, as if looking perplexed by some work of contemporary art, "You're just like her. You think you are special. Unique. That you deserve some-

Nighttime Kingdom

thing better by just existing. Well, I've got news for you," Ted Sr. would slur at Ted, "Everything you get in this life is what you work for, nothing is handed to you. Look at me," as he stumbled to his bed looking around the door frame around his room, "You think I asked for this? I was a sports star! I was the best athlete in all of Ohio during my year! What have you done? Nothing!" These exchanges would usually eventually culminate in Ted Sr. passing out and then being up and gone the next morning for his shift at the cannery. He would be long gone before Janelle and Ted awoke for school.

Those early mornings with Janelle were some of Ted's fondest of his childhood. Janelle, always a magnet for pop culture, would be in the bathroom styling and spraying her permed frosted hair to look like an 80s pop icon. Ted would sit on the toilet and watch her in the mirror for hours doing her makeup, bleaching the tips of her hair, or soft perming or ratting it, while saying things laughing like, "Higher the hair. Closer to God." It seemed at one point there was nothing but fluorescence and acid wash covering her entire body! She would glide through the horse barn like the adult child she had to be, wearing neon plastic bangles all the way up her wrists, while whistling and singing to Ted along with her Walkman. She handed Ted his lunch every day before school, with phrases like, "Totally tubular Mac n Cheese. Radical rice leftovers. Bodacious PB & J."

Every morning, she would pretend she was French and say, "Monsieur! Would you like some café au lait this morning?" before allowing Ted to drink coffee way too young, with way too much cream and sugar. When the weather was warm enough, they would sit outside on the patio in their pajamas before heading to school, laughing and talking about the gossip spreading through Hubert. "OMG did you see Shirley making out with Rob at the roller rink last Saturday?!" Janelle laughed.

To which Ted responded, despite having no idea who Janelle was really talking about, "Yeah she is such a whore," Janelle lamented, "Right? I can't believe her."

There was a cardinal's nest—the official bird of Ohio—nestled right up next to the porch where they sat and they would watch it as the seasons changed. The beautiful tan and red mother bird would set up shop, get settled, give birth to her chicks, and then bring them food before helping them out of the nest. Every season, the same mother bird would return. On occasion, Ted would say to Janelle, "Do you think she will ever come back? Do you think she ever thinks of us?" To which Janelle, ever the realist, would reply, "I doubt she will ever come back, kiddo. Do you blame her for dealing with him?" Ted knew, and usually didn't say anything, but just felt an overwhelming sense of sadness about it. Janelle would always quickly change the topic right after, "We are for sure getting that new LP today at the library, before stupid Shirley

Nighttime Kingdom

can get her hands on it. Come on, let's get you dressed for school. Life is waiting for us to explore, dance, and get crazy."

Rita never came back to Hubert, and they never heard from her again. Except once, right after Grandma Krieger died. She sent flowers with no card attached. The only time that Janelle and Ted saw her was on a live television broadcast live of a rally in Northern California, where a group of activists had chained themselves to a tree slated for demolition. Ted noticed she still looked beautiful, and pretty much the same. Different clothing, sure, but her demeanor was relaxed and she seemed confident in her own skin. That was pretty much it. No news before, and/or after. Just a hole in his heart which Ted felt and carried in him until he met Jerome in the summer of 1983.

Chapter 4
Sam & Ted

Ted arrived at the corner of Union Square and thought about stopping to see Sam at work. He always wanted to see him after having an episode. The most embarrassing aspect of his initial courtship with Sam was how the ghosts of his past managed to manifest themselves physically when they were first together. Sam represented to Ted the most vivid example of unconditional love. It was a liberating dance, weaving back and forth between wanting to let his guard down with Sam but also pushing him away as he did with anyone he felt close to. It made complete sense to Ted why he constantly played this push/pull dance of intimacy. Sam was unconditional. He did not know how to process or contend with such unconditionality. He was conditioned to be forever waiting for someone or something to change the terms of their arrangement. It wasn't his fault. It was how he'd learned, or rather was taught, to love as a kid. And as a teenager. It made sense he was terrified of what everlasting represented. It had led to complications between the two of them. Ted was terrified that if Sam really knew the truth about his past, he would leave.

Nighttime Kingdom

And it wasn't an unsubstantiated fear. Everyone up until Sam had left, or Ted would find out the hard way. He was playing a game with rules he did not know existed. To trust someone was one of the scariest propositions he could possibly contend with. In the past, it was easier to leave before, or not sustain, a real connection. It allowed him to be able to set the terms for his expectations. It is all so easy breezy until the wounds of the past start surfacing in an intimate relationship. In truth, most people could not handle his. It was too much. It was easier to pretend to be deep than to have to contend with the messiness that accompanies deeper intimacy with another person. Why would you want to? It is the most humbling thing anyone must deal with. Being a human being, that is. When any relationship moves past the honeymoon phase, a sour sun rises to usher in the ugly side of intimacy.

It is common knowledge that when you are first dating someone, you don't have a digestive system. You do not poop. You do not fart. Expelling gas simply doesn't happen in the honeymoon phase of love and sex. Well, Ted had long standing issues in his adult life with his digestion. At first, he just dismissed it as lactose-intolerance, and then too much coffee, sugar, alcohol, cigarettes, a gluten sensitivity, etc. You cannot just throw a bunch of different random things in your body like it were a garbage disposal and expect it to be fine, he reasoned. Because of these "difficulties" he had long maintained a strategic kinship and inner body map of all of Brooklyn and Manhattan's restrooms. If he were ever having an unexpected episode, he could then run off the train to the nearest bathroom. It was a humbling thing how, over the years and as he processed everything about his childhood and what'd happened to Jerome Hillcrest, that trauma arose and manifested in his body, especially in his nervous system. His body felt like it was constantly

31

at war with his mind. He wanted to exist, to pretend he was a functioning adult, but depending on his triggers it could derail him.

When the body has been shocked at an early age, the nervous system never fully recovers. There remains a lingering sensitivity that will surely manifest at the most inconvenient moments. One's fight-or-flight response having been triggered early on in life causes the lines between feelings of good nervousness—like love—and bad nervousness—like my body is telling me to get the hell out of here—to blur. It took many years for Ted to decipher this code and reliably differentiate between the two. The power of listening to your gut and intuition is that it is your spirit guide. When traumatic events and exchanges have rewired your fight-or-flight response, it is hard to figure out why your body is telling you to run while sitting across the table from somebody having a lovely meal. There is a real connection between the heart, lungs, stomach—and yes, colon—when it comes to the body's ability to relate to how we digest and process both actual food and drink and also life events. Suffice to say, it is beyond humbling when you are trying to just be chill and watch a movie on a first date but then must get up to unleash a bubbling torrent of IBS in someone else's toilet. He felt as usual his Grandmother Ruthie Krieger was speaking through him again. Don't get me wrong, Ted loved everything about food. The aftermath was the problem, and something he had to reckon with all the time these days.

When Sam and Ted met, food and exploring were the first things they really loved to do together. They would get off a train stop in an unknown neighborhood and walk and talk and then, when both were tired and hungry, stop and get something to eat or drink at a place that seemed like a local establishment. In many ways, Sam and Ted's courtship and romance was typical of many delusional NYC Friday to Sunday relationships. They would start on a Friday night with a drink, and then spend the weekend pretending they were going to live together and end up happily ever after. Except, in the story of Ted and Sam, they still talked to one after they parted ways on Sunday night.

Sam

The night of their second date, they decided to choose the F train and get off randomly at the Bergen stop. They headed off as usual, exploring the neighborhood right off Smith Street. At the time, it was just starting to be gentrified by custom high end boutique hat and bag stores and new wave record and coffee shops. Though the neighborhood still clung to some remnants of its most recent chapter of working class Italian immigrant residents, with some of their grocery stores and old restaurants remaining. Sam and Ted leisurely strolled, admiring all the brownstones that retained a sense of old Brooklyn and which did not seem as corrupted as the ones in Brooklyn Heights on the promenade. Oh, how that all seemed like a distant memory, presently being only accessible to those with generational connections to the previous owners, or generational wealth. Usually both.

They ended up stopping at an Italian café on the corner of Smith and Third, ordered a bottle of wine, and enjoyed appetizers. The conversation and night flowed by quickly, leaving both glowing and feeling enamored with one another and everyone around them. Sam, ever the optimist, confidently stated, "We're going to live right around here, you and me. And we are going to have a walk-up brownstone and live happily ever after." Ted thought to himself "God... this guy is laying it on thick, is he going to stab me later?" Deep down, though, he hoped Sam was being sincere and would text him back after letting him have all he wanted that night.

As it turns out, Sam was right about one thing. They would stay together. But he was wrong about the location of the brownstone. Ted and Sam ended up getting a deal on a brownstone off St. James's Place, in Clinton Hill. It was a totally different neighborhood, but still close, and at the time was still affordable. Bed Stuy was still regarded as a no-go zone among the majority of upwardly mobile, gay hipsters. This didn't bother Ted. He still had an adventurous streak to him after the confinement of growing up in Hubert, and loved the potential of a new neighborhood to explore and settle down in.

The one commonality between Sam and Ted was that they had similar fathers. Fathers who were completely emotionally distant, and who tried to beat the gay out of them. They both had a deep connection to one another and as a result understood why it was important to feel safe. That safety was robbed from the pair of them from a tender age and

Nighttime Kingdom

so both shared a need for trust to be re-established with every new adult relationship, at least with most. That early connection from childhood helped Ted feel safe with Sam from the very beginning. He noticed that instead of his body feeling a sense of nervousness, screaming at him to get out of there, it was relaxed. At first, Ted was not sure if Sam was really the one... he just felt so safe in his company, almost too safe, like he was with his current best friend Shantel. Friend zone territory. He was afraid that this dynamic that smelled more of friendship would squash the flames of good sexual intimacy. He was wrong. The connection was equal on both sides, and the rest was history. What a miracle it was to have met Sam and to have him in his life. Sam. The love of his life. His protector. His advocate. His forgiver. His soothsayer. Lover. Brownie maker. And, above all else, his family now that he had been away from Hubert for so long. Sam Klein. Oh, Sam! Lovable Sam. Bearish, huggable Sam. The Jewish grandmother. The father that Ted never had. After being in his presence, he did not know how he'd lived his life until that point without him.

The circumstances of their meeting was a curious and unexpected encounter. He'd been invited to go to a book release party by his best friend, Shantel Midnight. It was for an up-and-coming street artist who was known for putting stickers about sex positivity and the sexual revolution all over the Lower East Side and random places in Brooklyn. Looking back, it was hard to remember the name of that artist... but Sam would know. He always knew. That was Sam. He was dependable like that. And kind. And Thoughtful. And always able to read the temperature of a room, then adjust it as needed. What needed to shift. Who needed to stay. When it was time for someone else to go. Ted loved this the most about Sam. He was able to read people beyond words. It was a second sense or empathic quality that Ted had lost somewhere along the way. Most likely sacrificed at the altar of survival.

It was too much to be present and protected. Being present meant he had to feel everything. That was too much. He thought about this a lot when Pride was going on, or Coming out Days, when for the most part coming out was regarded as an act of bravery, a necessity, and a means to publicly empower yourself. Ted believed wholeheartedly in this idea—and embraced it—but always thought about the kids still in Hubert, like himself and Jerome. And then that whole mess of what happened. Sometimes the most revolutionary thing you can do or offer the world is simply taking care of yourself and living. Being brave and out was a wonderful thing, but if you lack the social or financial net to catch you, it is wiser to wait and find the right space to let your guard down to be exactly who you were meant to be.

Sam Klein represented that to Ted in so many ways. He admired how Sam would speak up and out in different social situations when someone said something homophobic, racist, or was in some other way unaware of the effect their words had on everyone else in the room. Sam was truly self-realized. It intimidated Ted early on in their courtship, but was also one of the reasons he fell in love with Sam. Besides the fact that in their first night together in bed, Ted felt for the first time he could let go. He'd never forget Sam fondly cuddling him from behind and whispering, "I am here. You are safe. I will protect you and not let anyone hurt you again." Unbelievable. It almost felt fake, too real, at first to Ted. "Is this guy serious? Is he a sociopath?!" It took a while for Ted to trust Sam in an intimate way. Sex was one thing. Intimacy was an entirely different can of worms.

Ted was standing in the entrance of Sam's office building in Union Square. Sam was born and raised in Long Island and

Nighttime Kingdom

oftentimes proudly labeled himself as a Gay, liberated, NYC Jew. It represented for Ted all the things he wanted and couldn't embrace back in Ohio. Unabashed confidence and pride in his sexuality, paired with a worldly and street-smart humorous attitude towards the world. Ted got into the elevator, pressed the 15th floor button for Brewster Publishers, and gently let out a sigh of relief. Sam was the touchstone when Ted started to have one of his episodes, but he was also aware of the reality that this weighed on Sam. He was already frayed at both ends with his job and social engagements and, at times, Ted grew worried and self-conscious about dumping and leaning on Sam so much more than he reciprocated such support.

The elevator doors opened and Ted approached the receptionist, a twenty-something hipster, who looked up from reading their magazine and stated condescendingly, "Can I help you? Have an appointment, I'm assuming?" This always annoyed Ted, given the fact that he stopped by more than twice a week to see Sam at work but was seemingly never remembered by —and therefore led to believe he never left any memorable impression on—this same receptionist. Ted cut back, "Yes, here to see Sam Klein, Ted Krieger." The receptionist typed in their computer, letting Sam know that Ted was waiting, and said, "He will come out and meet you if he has a second, he is in a meeting."

Ted turned, sat down in one of the waiting room chairs, and picked up his phone to see a text from Shantel, "Hey boo! Hope you are well, so excited to see you later tonight!" Ted put down his phone, overwhelmed and as usual avoiding Shantel because she always saw right through his bullshit in the best motherly type of way a friend could. Shantel Midnight and Ted had formed an immediate bond when they first met in an accelerated BA program at Pace almost twenty years ago. Ted was asked a question in their Intro to Psych class about his own relationship to the connection between early childhood experiences and coping mechanisms. As usual, his response was slow and too stunted for the professor's patience. Shantel was sitting across from him and replied, "I spoke with him earlier, and we were talking about how we have similar backgrounds coming from working class families and how that influenced an unhealthy way of recognizing, addressing, and coping with harm." Ted locked eyes with Shantel and mouthed a silent "Thank you." After that interaction, Shantel and Ted were the very best of friends.

Sam eventually emerged from the double glass doors in the waiting area and his eyes met Ted's.

"Hey! Didn't know you were stopping by... everything okay? Today is nuts because I'm preparing a presentation to meet with this new client. You know, the twenty-something career advisor of the century for their new book,"

Ted met him and gave in a hug and a kiss, "Yeah everything is fine, I just wanted to see you. Decided to take the afternoon off. Going to go shopping and make some apple turnovers for Shantel's engagement party, since she asked."

"Sounds great, I may be a few minutes late but will be there on time!"

Sam pressed the down button for the elevator and they locked eyes as it came to the surface and opened and they both stepped in. When the door closed, Sam relaxed.

"OMG I am so over this fucking place. Can you just give me a gun now?! I'm not sure I will make it."

Ted laughed, "Of course you will get through this! Listen, you are the strongest person I know. If you aren't going to make it, what does that say about me?" he said with a chuckle, while gingerly taking and leading Ted's hand towards his crotch.

Nighttime Kingdom

Sam hugged and pushed Ted's hand away as it landed on the ground floor, "Love you. See you later. Be nice to yourself."

Ted got out and turned to watch Sam waving and dancing in the elevator as the door closed like he was on a strip pole. He stepped out onto the street and started walking down Broadway, heading south towards Soho.

Chapter 5
Blue Ribbons

Grandma "Ruthie" Krieger's blue ribbons were her most cherished possessions. Each was proudly mounted atop the wood beam mantle over the fireplace of the horse barn, and each one was a badge of honor in the same way trophies are in sporting families.

Every entry category at the Apple Butter Festival had three tiers; first, second, and third place. There were also honorable mentions but, to be honest, any local who received an honorable mention would regard it as a backhanded insult. Honorable mentions usually went to the urban pioneer bakers who mystified and over inflated their egos in their kitchens to extend well beyond their skill set only to be met with insult when they didn't receive Best in Show Ribbons. Two tiers were above the categories awarded in each of the main categories. Those were Best in Division, such as apple butter or apple jam, and Best in Show.

Ruthie regularly garnered Best in Show for every Apple Butter Festival competition she entered, and the prize money was put to good use by the Krieger family, who struggled to keep the mortgage and taxes on the house paid. She continued

Nighttime Kingdom

to work until her death, cultivating the fields, diligently sowing, planting, and harvesting the apples each season. There was only ever one season she did not plant and harvest, and that was the year when her cancer had spread so widely that she could no longer walk the aisles. Though it did little to erode her determination, and she refused to derail her routines, including cooking and offering healing sessions to the townspeople. During the period after Rita left, Ruthie stepped in and was actively involved in caring for Ted. She felt it was important to pass down the knowledge and magic she'd gained from her father, Karl. She spoke only on occasion about "the gift" with Ted, including how only certain people had the gift of sight and that you needed to be careful how you used it and who you revealed your insights to.

Ruthie was a regular advisor at the Hillcrest Orchards each harvest season. She spoke with Ted at length about how to use your senses as the pathway to sight and using your gift, and often referred to the land spirits and the importance of listening and letting them be your wisdom guide to ensure a good harvest season. You could say there was a lot of superstition surrounding the transfer of knowledge and how to grow a good crop, as well as ensuring the right circumstances—that were always changing with the weather—to determine how much sun, wind, rain, and moisture would determine the variables for the season. Some farmers relied on the Farmer's Almanac. Ruthie didn't. She'd often say to Ted, "The real knowledge of everything we do is kept here inside, in our hearts, hands, bodies, that's where we keep the knowledge." Ruthie stepped in a great deal after Rita gave birth to Janelle and Ted. Janelle, always a free spirit, resisted Ruthie's side talks, but Ted was open and receptive. He was always by Ruthie's side, and had been for as long as he could remember. He was her little man, and had been absorbing her bodily knowledge from birth. Ted

Sr. couldn't care less. He would often comment on his mother's witchy knowledge, "Knock it off with this stuff, Ma. It is outdated and irrelevant," but Ruthie would just laugh.

Ruthie Krieger (nee Hepner) was born in the Rhineland of Germany, in 1934. Even as a child, she always was a symbol of good luck to her father despite the tragic death of her mother, Liza, in childbirth. Her father, Karl Hepner, loved to tell the story of immigrating to the US with young Ruthie, while she was still an infant in her blanket. They crossed the ocean together—from the vineyards of Germany to the New World—and he'd laid her down on the first apple tree he found outside of NYC when they landed.

Karl decided to immigrate to Hubert during a time of great political tension in Germany. Even though Karl was a German, he'd retained his knowledge of Yiddish and on occasion would speak broken Yiddish to the Amish community in close proximity to Middlefield, Ohio as they would come into Hubert to help build homes, additions, and a wide range of projects for the Hillcrest Orchard Corporation. By the time his wife, Liza, was pregnant with Ruthie he had already reached out to his sister about making his stake in the New World, even if it meant transferring his knowledge of harvesting grapes to apples. As soon as financially feasible, they booked their tickets on the next available steamer to set sail over the Atlantic to NYC. Liza Hepner was six months pregnant at the time. Four weeks later—with Karl blaming the stress of the long voyage—she went into early labor and died giving birth to Ruthie. "Ruthie and Ted carried this same hole in their hearts," Ruthie would say to Ted . He had her gift of sight. Though he didn't understand at the time, looking back it meant on a practical level that Ted was attuned to his senses and so could read people, the elements, and things around him with ease.

Both Karl's sister and her husband had already immigrated

to the United States and settled in Pittsburgh, so even though the strain of carrying a small child through the harrowing journey was considerable, he knew there was support to help him raise Ruthie upon arrival. Karl also knew there was work for him in the Dutch Pennsylvania and Ohio region, and had heard of the legendary plague of 1935 that'd annihilated most crops in the area. After skipping around from their landing in Ellis Island, they began following the long route through the farms of Dutch Pennsylvania and working along the way. Karl would work on an orchard for the season and then, relying on word of mouth, travel west to the next town and the next orchard that needed help. By the time they landed in Hubert in 1938, Hillcrest Orchards was still struggling against the plague that was decimating their operations by destroying almost half of the crop that season. Ruthie was four by then, and Karl knew she needed to be enrolled in a proper school. The need of Hillcrest Orchards met Karl's expertise and the desire for his daughter to have stability and a place to grow up.

Karl nicknamed Ruthie his little *Shenken* after that season, his little gift giver, and she carried that nickname most of her life. Ted and Janelle called her Mama Sken. But she went by Ruthie also. Sken or Ruthie. Depending on how you knew her.

"These recipes," she shared with Ted, "Were carried over in the hearts and hands of the immigrants, and passed down from one hand to another. They were never written on paper." She would take Ted's hand and hold it, saying slowly, "Hand to hand. Heart to heart. Heart to table. What I am giving to you was through my father to me. From his mother to him. For as long as we can remember. People have tried to take this from us. But no matter what people do to us on the outside, they will never be able to take away this," she said solemnly, pointing to her heart.

On Sundays, young Ruthie would cook with Ted, and on

occasion Janelle, for the family. She'd carry on and on about the inner family wisdom pertaining to growing and harvesting apples, and the spices for the blends of hops, cider, and baking traditions that were carried over from the Rhineland. When she was little, her father Karl did much the same thing. She would take Ted's hands and say, "This is it. The power is here. Your hands and your senses are all you need to heal both yourself and other people. May the love in my heart pass from these hands to you."

Ruth was the unofficial matriarch and healer of Hubert. Ted Sr. was consistently irked by what it involved, often coming home from his shift at the cannery to see someone in need of healing laid out on the kitchen table, "Mom you must stop this shit. It doesn't work, and this is what modern hospitals and doctors are for now." Ruthie would just nod in response, then quietly usher him out of the room. It did not matter. Her reputation for healing was solid among the folk of Krieger. It didn't matter what ailed them, she was the cure. Got an upset stomach? Some other malady? In need of a healing of the heart? They would say the same thing, "Go see Ruthie."

Ruthie told Ted that the reason people get sick can usually be traced to their heart; that all sickness stems from feeling trapped, stymied, or stuck in one's heart. She would say the feeling of being trapped is what brings about the slips, falls, inflammation and that people have lost sight of their senses and their hearts.

When people would stop by the house for treatment, Ruthie had Ted sit right beside her. At the time he was just tall enough to see the person laying on top of the ridiculous kitchen tablecloth of apples and ribbons, either face up or down, while Ruthie did a private consult. She would always start by sitting across from them and feeling their heart and pulse, before asking them questions about their digestion. Maybe this was

Nighttime Kingdom

where Ted first became obsessed and where his struggles with poop began? After the consult, she would have them sit up or lay down, and sometimes she would do a laying of the hands on areas that needed healing. When Mr. Wilson, the head foreman at Hillcrest Cannery, stopped by one day Ted remembered she took his hand and placed it over Mr. Wilson's, then said "See? Do you feel how this part is cold and this part is warm? What this means is that the connection points are stunted. We need to figure out how to get the energy flowing again to the rest of this hand." Afterwards these examinations she would either scurry into the spice room to make a specific tea concoction for the person to drink, or she would make a wrap using cheesecloth to place over their wounds, arthritis, or area of inflammation. Ruthie also spoke a great deal about the evils of sugar—especially white sugar—and claimed that sugar was what would bring the whole Earth down. She would say "Sugar is the devil." At which point Janelle would always sigh, through a mouthful of sugary cereal, while sitting next to Ted and rolling her eyes. Ruthie's laments often went along the lines of, "The sweetness in the fruit is all you need to make a wonderful apple pie. It is really listening to the timing of when the apples are ripest and bringing out their sweetness while cooking. That is more necessary than sugar. When people use a lot of sugar it is a lazy rushing of the process instead of listening to what the apples want to do."

Janelle would say things to Ted to try to ruin his spirit like, "You know she is a Valium addict, right? And at one point Dad was considering putting her in a mental hospital." Ted didn't care. He thought she was the sweetest, most caring person he knew. She was real. And he got it. Her sensitivity to the world was both a blessing and a curse. When she was at her best, she was a healer... but at her worst, she was a destroyer. He knew that all too well.

William J. O'Brien

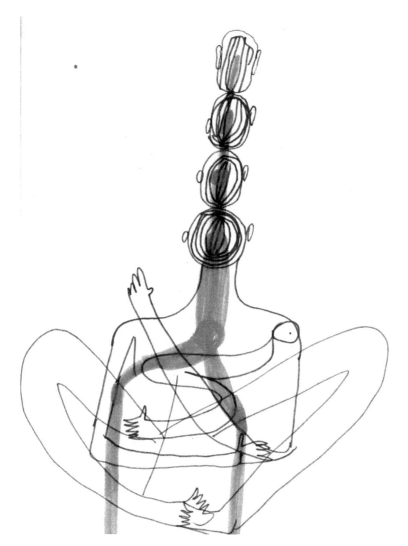

The healer

Ted also learned how to cook from Ruthie. She possessed no written recipes or measuring cups, and would guide Ted through all the recipes that her father Karl gave to her by intuition alone. Important variables like the right time to core the apples, use the cider, pour the lemon juice in, boil the mixture,

Nighttime Kingdom

simmer the apples for, and roll out the dough could not be reduced to a cheap formula for her. She just used her hands. Ted would watch as she gauged how many apples, how much flour, butter, and the temperature needed as if she were playing a cello concerto by heart. Coordinating the hand with the knife. Rolling and kneading with the inside of her palm. He'd watch her do these things in awe, all the while hanging on her every word as she imparted wisdom, like, "You need to move your wrist in a circular fashion, at first fast and then slow, gently letting it rest." It was always magic, from beginning to end. She would have Ted smell the air, "Do you smell that? Good, that means the apples are starting to ferment and most people think it is time to stop cooking here. They are incorrect. You want to go just a bit further, until you can see the natural sugar and juices forming on top." Ted would nod his head, obediently listening, "Now, slowly use the back of this wooden spoon and scoop and flatten the apples. Not too hard, but enough that they start to fold and compress into the batter."

It was all magic to Ted. All of it. He was endlessly proud whenever they finished anything. Pies. Turnovers. But his favorite was always making apple butter. He loved boiling and sterilizing the jars. He loved the snapping of the lids when they were done. He especially loved the weeks leading up to the Apple Butter Festival, when Ruthie would drag an old family cauldron outside and make a batch over an open fire that could feed a hundred people. It felt so magical. It was so comforting. Until it stopped. Until Ruthie died. The only time he started to cook again was for the Apple Butter Festival of 1983. It was just too hard. Too painful. Unbearable.

At dawn and dusk, Ruthie would bring Ted to the orchards, sometimes as early as 3:30 am when she was asked to offer her consulting magic about what needed to happen during the harvest season. Ted felt this was his first schooling in the fields, well before real school learning, and it was an altogether different curriculum. It was an education in the ways of seeing, hearing, touching, and sensing. She would say, "The dawn is for listening, and the dusk for appreciating. The time between dusk and the dawn is the time when the human world and the spirit world communicate. Best to close your mouth and listen."

Before she did anything in the fields, and before commencing a healing or cooking a meal, she would sit or stand as upright as she could. She said to Ted that, "This part is most important. Stand with your feet on the ground and be as tall as you can imagine. Imagine you are a tree. Imagine your spine being the same as the roots and trunk. Stand up straight, as much as you can, and let your muscles and hands be as relaxed as possible by your sides." Swaying from side to side, her gray hair blowing in the breeze, she'd continue, "Now, breathe. Breathe as if you are going down as far as you can into the soil. As if you are the ground itself. Now, when you inhale, sway your body upwards as if your head is like heaven." She talked about the connection of the feet as being a part of the Earth, "It gives us strength, but it also is where we place the bad. If we treat the soil and respect it the right way, it can take our wounds, our pain, all the bad and transform it into the beautiful again." After breathing, she would raise her hands, palms almost together but ever so slightly apart, and feel the wind between them, "Feel this." She would then offer her gratitude to the land spirits, "Guide us. Give us clues, and if we do not listen, lead us back to your way, teach us and we will listen." Afterwards, she would walk to the bark of the tree and touch the branches and the apples. "See? This, Ted, this means the tree wants to be fed or the tree is sick," She'd then proceed to rub another concoction she'd made in the kitchen and add water with some cheesecloth over the surface. Regardless of whatever people said, Ruthie's concoctions worked. The next

Nighttime Kingdom

day, the workers would remove the cheesecloth and the tree's skin would be healed and producing a new branch and, most likely in a few months, a delicious apple.

It was morning when Ruthie died. Ted found her. Janelle was with him, and they'd just come back from school. She was sitting in the same rocking chair that she'd held Ted in as a baby and sung to him and told him the stories of the Rhineland and the tall tales of her past. Ted crawled up on her lap and held her hand and said to Janelle, "I'm going to bring her back," holding his hands above her heart, "See? Just like she taught me." Janelle tried taking him off, but Ted refused. He just kept screaming, "I know. I know how to do it. Like she taught me," repeatedly. He held her hand. It took over two hours for Janelle and Ted. Sr. to get him off her body. It felt like the longest afternoon of his life.

Chapter 6
Country Boy

Wounds inflicted at an early age take decades to scar over, and even longer to heal. There is a fuzziness that is necessary to function in the interim. Such numbness dulls the edges of the pain. The edges of the anxiety. The sensations of the body that haunt you when you sense it resurfacing.

When Ted first landed in the city, he was directed to stay with one of Janelle's friends she'd met at jazzercise camp the summer that Rita left. Janelle tucked a small note in Ted's pocket as he was about to board the Greyhound. It was the day after graduation from Hubert High.

"Promise me," she said pulling him close, like she was going to bite his ear, "That you'll call Lisa as soon as you get there. She lives in her parent's rent-controlled apartment on the Upper West Side, and she said you could stay with her as long as you like."

"I will."

"Promise?"

"Yes, I promise."

Nighttime Kingdom

Denim stitched jeans. Brown worker boots. Flannel shirt. Fresh off the bus. Or train. Or maybe having hitched a ride to the city from the nearest midwestern town within 100 miles. A younger version of Ted, like a reflection from twenty years ago, walked past him and brushed his shoulder as he crossed Bleecker into Soho. Subtle gestures. Clues. His identical twin, though twenty years younger, was getting off the bus in Times Square. Up and down Broadway. North and South on the Avenues. East and West. The villages of sex. Walks of shame. Moments of pride. Wide eyed. Mystified. Curious. The first chapter of his new life. Partially terrified, but fully alive. No more hiding.

This was his favorite part of the city: a mix of active pedestrian life with stores that were affordable, cafes, and art movie theaters that still existed and showed real independent art films. He texted Shantel, "I'm going to make apple turnovers tonight for your party," Shantel responded, "OMG thank you! So excited!! I appreciate you!"

There were so many different stores to look at from the strip of Union Square, up through Soho, Noho, Tribeca, and all the way down to Chinatown. He loved the variety and wild juxtaposition of it all. One window might contain antique clocks and watches, a few doors down there would be a soft-core porn coffee table bookstore that was wedged in right beside a place to buy specialized hats, right next to a fast-food place, and beside it a place to buy high-end Japanese toilets... heated seats and warm water bidets! He loved all of it, and wondered if he would forever remain a wide-eyed country boy in the city. It didn't sound so bad.

He reminisced but also cringed while walking past the restaurant where he'd had his first real gay date. A sushi spot. He did not know what sushi was, or how to use chopsticks. What was being a vegan? Then he strolled past the bar he'd gone to after telling his friends he was going home. He'd stayed there till the early hours, cruising for his next May to December romance. Unsuccessfully. Next was the intersection where he'd bought his first designer shirt, with his whole paycheck. Then the café where he'd waited for his third date with Sam, with his cappuccino. Designer scarves. High end athletic shoes intended for the mountains, but which only saw the streets of Chelsea. Lonely. But never desperate.

NYC was like Hubert. Class tensions. The haves with the have nots.

He was still the same little kid that resisted being potty trained. Who peed and pooped outside in Hubert, by a tree, until kindergarten. Who wore Rita's maxi-pads in his underwear to avoid going inside to go to the bathroom. Somehow he was presently walking out of high-end stores with his boutique bags. Though remnants of his past in Hubert still cropped up in unexpected places. You can take the boy outta the country, but taking the country outta the boy ain't so simple. Like when a new boutique fried chicken place that used corn flakes and had farm to table apple pies made him roll his eyes. Grandma Krieger would die laughing if she saw them plating the apple pies and then coming with a blow torch to finish the caramelizing of the apples at each table!

Theater opening. Prix fixe... say what?

He was the same kid who never saw a dentist till he was eighteen, and was now walking past the high-end dental salon that'd capped and fixed his teeth when he got his first job with dental insurance. The hygienist hovering over his mouth had shouted, "Cancel all my appointments for the rest of the afternoon. I do not know how I am going to begin to deal with this, but here you are... and here I am... and let's try to remove all this crud."

Ted was so proud of both himself and Shantel. Just two

young queer kids that broke on through to the other side of the doors. Shantel was getting engaged to the sweetest boy from Connecticut. He'd probably tricked with a friend of his father ten years ago before he caught the train at Grand Central. He was still surviving, but Shantel was thriving. They had an amazing condo overlooking the Hudson, in a building... with a doorman! It was the same type of building that Shantel and Ted would enter through the back elevator to turn tricks to pay the rent all those years ago, but now they were a senior executive partner at a major advertising firm! Yes indeed, they'd come a long way. Catching his reflection in the window of his favorite baking shop, Ted saw the NYC version of himself. Prim and Proper. Contained. All cleaned up... maybe even classy?

Grandma Krieger always said that they were descended from royalty, and Janelle would whisper to Ted, "You know she only says that to give us hope that we'll escape from this hellscape." He passed now. Unnoticeable. He learned the urban rules of neurotic speed walking. Decisiveness. Where to turn, go left. Now right. Down the steps. Transfer lines. Move all the way into the car. Tourists and newbies always linger in the front too long. He'd adopted the accumulated impatient urgency at restaurants when ordering food and no longer balked at prices but inside cried for his bank account. Like an adult.

"Excuse me," Ted walked past the tourists blocking most of the sidewalk and past the overflowing dumpster, making his way into the alley towards the entrance of his favorite baking store off Broome St. Would *Country Ted*—as Shantel nick-named him—know or find this place twenty years ago? I think not. You were here if you were a local baker. Or restaurant owner. Or true, underground foodie. No newbies here. He was in. He'd found the right language that sealed his membership to the city.

Small bits of gray here or there. Passing.

He opened the door. He knew the owner, Tom, and greeted him jokingly, "Bonjour," before perusing the aisles. Ted was so proud of Shantel. They'd met young, and grown up together in the city. He knew their good sides. Their messy sides. The beautiful sides of Shantel. He knew the real Shantel. Shantel had taught Ted how to walk the streets of NYC. She/they contained the gift of sight. Same as Ted. Same As Ruthie Krueger. When to shift, listen, and respond to her surround-ings. Cutting through the city's rough and gritty edges took a certain something. Finding the classy soft edges and cores did, too. And it was possible even in the worst neighborhoods. They/she knew where to go. They knew when to leave. When to plant a seed, let it grow, and nurture it. And when to let those seeds die. When to close a connection or switch trains to another car. When it was safe to sit longer and lock eyes with a cute stranger. Who was safe and who not to take home if you

Nighttime Kingdom

hoped to see tomorrow. Yes, Shantel was the definition of chosen family to Ted. Shantel took Ted under their wing. Incubated and nurtured the fledgling gay NYC Ted from his country bumpkin shell. In the first few years that Ted had moved to the city, although he slept with guys, he was not officially out. And never *ever* kissed anyone on the lips. All exchanges were in dark alleys. Under stalls. In the basements of bars with back rooms. Gym saunas. Dingy locker rooms. All while avoiding any eye contact. And, above all else, there were no second connections. Easy. Clear. Direct.

He'd worked a few odd jobs, both as a dishwasher and bartender, and in the few days and nights and with whatever money he still had left had started taking night classes at Pace. The sidewalks were, as Shantel stated with their finger pointing from east to west, "They're for everyone to claim. Our space. They have the swanky buildings and doormen. But this is ours," while strutting through the West Village hand to shoulder with Ted on that monumental first night. The first night he officially went out to gay bars.

But Shantel was not always Shantel. As Ted was not always Ted. She/they were born in East Harlem, but like Ted had contended with being born into poor circumstances. They were determined to rewrite their narrative as an adult. Ted had met Shantel a few years after they transitioned, and never asked about their childhood. Sometimes it came up, though, and information was provided... what their dead name was. Where they were born. Information about their mother or father. All of it was dead, as far as they were concerned. Bits and pieces would come out here and there, especially on holidays or at Christmas, while together in their small studio apartment in Harlem. It'd come haltingly, greased with alcohol, "Little Enrique used to live just around the block from us, you know," they'd slur, while crying, "You know, his family, mother, father... live only a block away from here... they walk past me and pretend I am a total stranger."

Shantel also brought Ted to the balls in the Bronx. He would sit on the toilet and watch her get ready, just like he'd done with Janelle. Then Ted would watch Shantel perform in the balls. She had the same ribbons and trophies lined up in the living room, like Grandma Krieger back in Hubert. Only the categories were different, Best in *Face*, *Femme Queen*, and *Realness*. Shantel had nicknamed Ted their *Country Boy*, and joked about wearing the original outfit he wore when he arrived from Hubert for the ball. As it turns out, he walked in the category for, *Fresh off the Boat* with his *Country Boy* realness outfit. And won. It was a joke. But he still had a trophy. A gay trophy.

After going to the balls and coming home, Ted and Shantel would cook together for all the misfits and stragglers that would crash at their small studio. This meant sometimes five or six young kids were curled up on a mattress for the night. Small moments of chosen family. It started with butter. And they would make food for all the kids with whatever they had. Shantel would joke with Ted, pulling her legs up on their cardboard folding table, "these legs are made from butter. The finest. All the way from Paris. They started to cook together from memory, with the recipes they remembered by heart in those early mornings in the dawn, just like Ted had done with Ruthie. And it was bittersweet, as those painful points of the past he'd left in Hubert collided with the real adult he'd become in NYC.

Shantel was also the only person who knew about what happened with Jerome and Ted, all those years ago back in Hubert. When Ted told the story about Jerome, she didn't blink an eye or look. She remained totally unfazed, wiping the tears from his cheeks and offering, "Ted, the wounds of our past follow us, no matter where we go. They hang like loose threads that tug at our heart as reminders of things we left behind and tried to forget... the transition from boy to man, or girl to woman, or boy to girl/boy, or girl to boy/woman, or a forever changing and beautiful balance of back and forth can be some of the most painful chapters. We start seeing things we do not want to see in our bodies. The people around us point out how we do not behave or act like a boy or girl should..." she trailed off, before sighing and turning towards him and looking him in the eye, "And the people closest to us see this, and that hurts us even more. For me, it was my step-father. For you it was your father, for Jerome it was his father. Some of us eventually must run and grow up on the streets, since we couldn't handle what happened to us every night under the sheets. Often our own fucking parents—who were supposed to raise and protect us— are those who abuse us," she lovingly touched Ted's cheek and wiped another tear away, "And some of us make it through. We survive. Some do not. It is nothing to do with our strength. Just the circumstances of survival. But we are here now, at this cheap ass folding table, and we are going to share a meal together."

When you are young, and harm occurs, you do not have the tools or language to adequately articulate that pain. As adults, the work is then to speak to that harmed child and bridge the gaps so healing can start to occur. Space must be made for the inner child to be listened to. The inner child must be given a voice. Only through allowing the inner child to speak can the adult find lasting peace from the past. The path towards healing is one on which the inner child is permitted to speak, to guide us, and lead us to the areas in ourselves that were hidden, neglected, or forced into cocoons because those around us feared who we were inside. The shackles of being a man are placed on boys from an early age. They are trained not to feel. Or show emotion. Or reveal vulnerability. Because that is gayness. And that is fundamentally bad. A silent code. Weakness is gay. Crying is gay. Showing affection towards other men is gay. The only thing that is gay is the stereotypes of men. The idea of what maleness is becomes generationally reinforced. It is a construction that is handed down. Except it is not handed down. It is dropped. And these constraints are heavy. Their pressures are crushing, and many think the answer is to crush others. This is what causes violence.

Walking down the aisles of the store, he became overwhelmed with emotion and started to cry. Maybe the things in the past sometimes have a silver lining that is not always filled with pain and regret? He picked up two of his favorite wrapped bars of butter from Paris and put them on the counter. Apple turnovers. Yes. That's what it was going to be.

Chapter 7
Seeds

To restrain one's own heart does nothing to stop the desires of the flesh from burning.

When you grow up poor, you really don't know it. Not until someone tells you. Or makes you feel different or unwelcome in some way. It can occur in small gestures. A glance. A snide comment. A tone. An insinuation. At first, it almost comes across as confusion. Shock. Then there's a feeling that follows. The first one is commonly embarrassment, then it warms into shame, simmers into jealousy, and sometimes even boils into anger.

For the most part, Ted was a happy and content child during his early life in Hubert. He did not notice he was poor or uncultured until it was pointed out to him in small ways. Who got a hot lunch, and why? What you brought in your lunch was a big part of it. The kids with the deer meat and apple butter sandwiches were the cannery kids. Who got to be able to buy a special extra sweet snack from the snack lady contributed to this calculus, as did if you could afford to eat pizza on pizza day. So did who was able to go on field trips.

Who had a television. And who bought new clothes and school supplies at the beginning of each year. Then there was Christmas. The kids whose parents worked at the factory knew if the harvest year was good or not by how much Santa came to town. It did not go unnoticed that the kids whose parents were lawyers or doctors *always* had Santa visit. But it was more than gifts and who had a television. It was also who had clean clothes and bathed every day. Who was taught to floss and brush their teeth.

Someone always notices a smelly kid, or one with lice. Then someone laughs. Then the teacher says something like, "Be quiet!" and then you're instructed to go the nurse's or principal's office. Then, despite not being in trouble, it feels like you are in trouble. Was that the teacher exhibiting subtle disgust? Pity? Or, worse, indifference? Still, at least you aren't the only one. When you're a poor kid, there exists a silent bond between you and others who also are. Kinda like being gay. In amidst your collective shame, there is also pride and solidarity.

Young Ted

Nighttime Kingdom

Grandpa and Grandma Krieger had been babysitting Janelle and Ted, since Rita and Ted Sr. wanted to travel to Akron for a concert at the coliseum. There was always a seasonal catalog from the local national department store in the living room. Though it wasn't often ordered from, it was heavily used for dreaming of the things they wanted, especially Janelle. The few times it was used was for ordering the most basic, most practical necessities that one cannot find in a small, rural town located so far from department stores. As a young kid, Ted came across the male underwear section of the catalog and was enamored by all the handsome models in different types of under and pajamas. He was curious, fascinated, and attracted to their muscular physiques. It was a natural and curious attraction he felt towards the men modeling on the glossy color pages. They were so perfect looking. Perfect hair. Nice skin. Everything Ted hoped he would look like as a grown man.

"What in the hell are you doing, Ted?" he heard Grandpa Krieger boom, hovering over him momentarily before snatching the catalog from Ted, "I don't want to ever see you ever looking at this ever again!"

Ted was mortified. He didn't understand what he'd done wrong. The men in the catalog looked just like him. When you grow up in an environment that sends you messages daily that who you are and who you are attracted to is wrong, it becomes difficult not to hide every facet of that side of you from everyone. This is especially true if you are a gay kid. Or just a kid who does not fit perfectly into the binary mold of gender stereotypes. Your parents will dress you appropriately, but cargo shorts and polo shirts only go so far... your mannerisms, demeanor, and social expressions always reveal who you really are inside. Expressive hand movements. Laughing too loud. Walking a certain way to line up for gym class. It was a painful performance, and one that had to be repeated daily, imitating how boys were supposed to act. Ted always wondered if it was how it was for everyone... did everyone have to pretend?

Ted's childhood room was the exact size of a horse stall, because it was once a horse stall in a different life. Few clues remained of that past, except the wood paneling on the walls that met up with the drywall that created an enclosed space. The door was also still the original sliding door, and the metal hooks that were the originals. Ted sometimes had dreams about the horses inside, and woke up wondering if they were ghosts of the past tenants coming back after their slaughters to get revenge. But Ted loved that room, and the small hidden crawl space in the back of his closet. The closet had a normal enough looking front section, with a metal bar holding up his clothes on hangers and a space for his shoes underneath. Further back there was a slight step upwards to another space that was slanted where the ceiling came down on one end. It was just enough height for someone to sit, and lay down if necessary, but not stand towards the back. It was a perfect space for just one or maybe two people to comfortably sit back there. He decorated the inside with discarded Christmas lights and arranged decorations along the four different corners of the walls all the way to the top of the ceiling in rows, so it felt like sitting underneath his own tree of light. There was not room for much inside the crawl space, except for a blanket and a pillow, but Ted would pin up pictures of all sorts of different types of birds that he saw in the backyard and clipped out from catalogues, as well as pictures of the different types of apples he learned about in the orchards.

That catalog incident with Grandpa Krieger left a permanent impression on young Ted. It was clear that what he wanted and desired was not right under the guise of certain eyes, so knew he had to conceal his attraction to men. But the

Nighttime Kingdom

crawl space in the back of his closet was his, and only his. It was a secret chamber inside the rigidly regimented, heteronormative hell of Hubert. A secret sanctuary within the hangover of a horse stall within a makeshift home. Ted had few other spaces that felt they were for him. Though the library was one. Ted and Janelle would go and camp out at the library most days after school and curiously go through books, records, and items they could find to allow dreams of places outside of Hubert to grow. He would also draw in the art room at school during recess and free time and anytime that was designated as work. On occasion, he would hide items in his desk and locker at school. Although these were technically public spaces, they were not safe spaces for Ted. They were public spaces for the Hubert version of Ted. For the fake outer shell he had to act out, not for the person he truly was on the inside. The Perfect son, who was going to get married—of course that meant a woman, that wasn't even a question—and start a family and stay in town. Pass down all the expectations from one generation to the next. It was not like the catalog incident did anything to stop Ted from being attracted to boys, or the handsome quality of the men he saw in the fashion magazines mailed to their house. What it did change was his self-awareness of showing publicly that he was attracted to other boys. This hyper awareness and skill in hiding and concealing those desires from everyone around him grew. Ted Sr. always seemed like he was sniffing around Ted, like a dog rooting out his scent to check if he was the right alpha male or not.

And so it was that he became fractured. A duality in his identity formed. A schism opened. An image was constructed to publicly hide who he was, only to be removed in private. Only then would he allow himself to be himself. Just a normal boy who happened to like other boys. Ted would watch the mail to see when the new catalogues would arrive.

William J. O'Brien

Some were planned. Others random marketing advertisements. He would grab the mail, and usually Janelle would say, "Chill! It's okay, just take what you want, unless it's mine. Then it's off limits." He would scurry back to his secret cove, embed himself behind the racks of clothes, and with a dim flashlight cut out the men he was most attracted to. He'd give them names, create backgrounds and backstories and characters and paste them into an old baby scrapbook for Ted that Rita had left behind from his childhood that had gone unused. In the sections where it said *baby's first tooth,* or *baby's first steps,* he would paste down an image from the catalog and write their names beside it. He also drew speech balloons between them, as if they were talking and had a relationship. John with sandy brown hair, Jose with beautiful eyes, Trenton with muscles. On the nights when Rita and Ted Sr. would be having one of their annual explosive fights, he would crawl inside the space with his pillow and small flashlight and fall asleep with his book of crushes and admirers.

To Ted's knowledge, no one knew about this book. No one except Janelle. That discovery of hers had been made by mistake. She was looking for her curling iron and screaming at Ted, "Look, little dude, I know you have it! And I don't care, I just need to look good for Shirley's party!"

As she pushed the clothing aside in the closet with her hands, "Where is it, shrimp?" Ted quickly tried to hide the book, but Janelle grabbed it from him, "Look at what we have here, little secrets book, huh little brother?" Ted pleaded, desperately scrabbling at Janelle's hands to grab it back, "Please don't Janelle I mean it. Please don't open it." Then Janelle opened the book, and her expression quickly changed when she saw all the cutouts of the male underwear models with hearts and bubble captions communicating with each other. Ted

64

started to tear up and cry, "Please don't tell anyone, Janelle, especially Dad. I will be in big trouble."

THE BOX INSIDE OF A BOX

Janelle sat down in the small area step within the closet, wriggled in closer to Ted, and brought his cheek to her chest, "Little man, there is nothing to be ashamed of here. As my friend said at the pizza party last night, you love who you love. And that is what it is. Everyone likes different pizza toppings. Your favorites are your favorites. But pizza is pizza."

"Love you, Janelle."

"Love you too, little brother, I truly do. And for just who you are. Now, you gonna hand over that curling iron, or what?"

After that, Ted knew that Janelle was truly his protector. Though that didn't change his habits or paranoia around the town of Hubert or at school. That fear was omnipresent for him. In the boy's bathroom, Ted kept his gaze facing rigidly forward as if he were staring down a gun. Just a slight glance, even out of innocent curiosity, and someone might notice. He would be pegged as a fag then, and therefore a target from that point on for their ridicule. Keeping eyes straight ahead at the urinal was one thing he could do, but one thing that was unavoidable was another boy catching his eye. Try as he might not to be, he'd become enamored with and mystified by another boy every now and then. He couldn't hide his desires. He would overcompensate with his own interests, like most boys being obsessed with their hobbies, and the usual rough and tumble. Ted genuinely liked the same things too, but would overcompensate by being more aggressive in the pushing and shoving on the playground and in any intimate interactions with the other boys so as to avoid suspicion. But with Ted Sr. he just did not have the energy, or maybe he just did not care about trying to hide it from him. Ted Sr. was an athlete and obsessed with football, so naturally Ted was required to play. It was as painful and awkward as any intimate interaction between the two of them could and always would be. Ted Sr. would try to teach him to run and intercept a quarterback like he'd done at his age. Then Ted, with all his effort, might try to coordinate, run, and tackle the pretend dummy set up in the backyard. But he never quite got it. His father's disgust and disappointment was palpable. *My son is a faggot.*

Ted learned to separate and compartmentalize who he desired growing up as a child from the role that he was playing for the town of Hubert. It was just like his mother had done, except in Ted's circumstances he didn't have the option of escaping. He thought about running away after Rita left. In the back cave of his closet, he packed a runaway bag and thought of the right circumstances to allow him to escape and be reunited

Nighttime Kingdom

with her. Perhaps he would stow away in one of the Hillcrest Cannery trucks at night, and at the first stop he'd sneak off to the nearest phone and look up Rita Krieger in the phone book. Then she would pick up the phone and rush to save him. Then he would be free. Finally free.

Chapter 8
The Kingdom

After having lived your entire life on guard, waiting for the next hit or impact, you cannot expect your heart to just relax. After all, it only survived this long because it didn't.

Ted had known of Jerome Hillcrest since they were in the same kindergarten class. Son of the Hillcrest dynasty, born to current heir Greg Hillcrest, he was already widely known within the school. He was destined for popularity, since all the other parents in the class wanted their kid to be friends with their boss's kid. It was a no brainer. If our kids are friends, we can be friends. Then he will promote me from factory to corporate. Pretty simple.

Ted noticed Jerome, but avoided him and frankly regarded him as a bit annoying and coddled by the world. They existed in separate friend groups and different worlds. In elementary school, Jerome always had money to buy snacks from the snack lady and get pizza whenever he wanted. He'd go on trips around the world. From the outside, he represented to Ted everything he did not have and probably would never have in his lifetime. And it wasn't just the money. Ted was relegated to

Nighttime Kingdom

outcast status, while Jerome was encircled by jocks. Ted was a freak. Jerome was a jock. By the time their junior year of high school rolled around, the different planets they inhabited had begun spinning in entirely different orbits. Though Ted didn't mind being on the fringes, even if those were some lonesome walks down the halls. He gained inspiration from all the books, magazines, and art films that he would check out at the library. He would sit on the free school computer and find any company that would send free items, books, or samples and look forward every day to checking his mailbox. Every day, after school he would gather his horde for the day—miscellaneous catalogues, samples, and cassettes—from the mail and go into the back of his closet to listen to music, read, draw, and build on decorating the mystical world he'd been building since he was a kid. Since Rita left. By the time his junior year arrived, the secret chamber in the back of that horse barn had grown into a mystical world of gods and goddesses, cutouts, and drawings of different celebrities he admired. But all his most sacred secrets and desires were always hidden in Rita's baby book. That baby book contained all the things he loved, was afraid to ask for, and was the vessel that symbolized the things that he'd lost, and what he longed for in their absence. Under a small piece of wood was where Ted stowed away the baby book for safe keeping at the end of each day.

It was the last week of the eleventh grade when Jerome and Ted ended up in detention together. To this day, no one knows for sure who threw the smoking cigarette into the trash can that set the fire in the boy's bathroom. Both Jerome and Ted were coincidentally using the stalls at opposite ends of the room and had no idea the other was there. When panicked voices and pattering feet and the slamming of the door filled the air, along with the smell of smoke, both Ted and Jerome emerged. It was already too late. Mr. S. had entered the bathroom, and passed his verdict based on proximity alone. Both of them were guilty. Given Jerome's status at Hillcrest, they were only scolded at the time but were additionally required to attend detention the following Saturday. Ted Sr. didn't find out about the incident from Mr. S. No, Greg Hillcrest called him on the phone of the cannery factory floor to have a chat... and you can likely imagine the shit storm that was unleashed on Ted that evening in the kitchen. He was pulled aggressively from his secret lair by his father and immediately slapped across the face. "You listen here, kid, don't you fuck up everything for me. Whatever shit you got into with Jerome Hillcrest ends now. Do not talk to him ever again." Ted, still feeling the burning from his father's palm in his face, collapsed into bed. He held back the tears for as long as he could. Only once Ted sr. left did he allow himself to weep into his pillow for the rest of the night.

The day of detention was uneventful, at least for the most part. Ted showed up early, at 7:30 am, to Mr. S.'s classroom. Jerome was already waiting at the front desk. Ted took his place and Mr. S. came strolling in, casually proclaiming, "Gentlemen, welcome to Saturday detention. You are mine for the next four hours." Jerome and Ted's eyes met, both with the same curious and afraid and dumbfounded look in them. Mr. S. led them to a janitorial room down the hall and handed Ted a bucket with a sponge and soapy water and Jerome a metal tool to scrape dirt and grime and gum off surfaces. They walked down the steps to the lower-level basement, right in front of the cafeteria, to a wall that was used by the juniors and seniors to lounge in between classes and lunch. On the wall was one of the biggest concentrated areas of disposed bubble gum that Ted had ever seen.

"Okay gentlemen, time to get to work! I'll come back to check on you periodically." Mr. S. left and Ted and Jerome exchanged nervous glances.

Nighttime Kingdom

"Well guess we should get to work," sighed Ted.

"I am not supposed to do this type of work. This is what the help is for."

"Yeah, well, you are the help now, buckaroo. Time to get to pushing this bucket of soap!"

What happened next was an accident. He truly hadn't meant to splash water all over Jerome's polo shirt. Jerome looked at him for a second, then splashed him back. Before long, they were both covered in soap and laughing hysterically.

Jerome

After school was over for the year and Ted had just turned seventeen, he started his first job at the Hillcrest orchards. This

consisted of cleaning up all the dropped leftover apples, taking care of trimming the trees and bushes, and moving and feeding the animals in the family barn. Picking up the discarded apples meant meandering along the rows of the orchards with a wheelbarrow and then trundling them back to the stables and feeding them to the pigs, horses, and cows. The responsibility of tending to the soil around the roots of the apple trees was also his, as was wrapping the branches for healing like he'd learned from Grandma Krieger. There were also a few odds and ends that needed to be handled on the Hillcrest property which he saw to. Nothing exciting, and altogether uneventful for the most part. Although he would see Jerome from time to time. They would keep their distance and avoid contact, but eventually that silence was broken one day when Ted slipped a note to Jerome when he was doing his annual daily tour of the property with Greg Hillcrest and the head foreman.

What follows is a series of letters that were written between Ted Krieger and Jerome Hillcrest, at the beginning of that summer.

June 8th, 1983

Jerome, Super cool to see you the other day in the fields with your Dad! Sucks that we are not supposed to talk with one another after the bathroom incident. Sort of hard not to though, isn't it? Like, we see each other every day! Have you heard any new intel on who did it? Annoying that we were blamed for something we didn't do, right? How is your summer break going so far? Doing anything cool with your free time? I'm pretty much just working, then going home

Nighttime Kingdom

and listening to records and watching movies from the library. My sister, Janelle, has a crush on this guy... Fred? I think that's his name. He's the quarterback from your team, know him? If you are interested, maybe write me back and leave it under the big rock by Aisle 2, Row 6, Tree 7.

Cool to hang in detention last month together. Mr. S. can be so weird. Anyways I'll check the rock at Aisle 2, Row 6, Tree 7.

Ted

~

June 12th, 1983

Hey man,

Thanks for the note! I've always wanted a pen pal! Just joking.

Looks super cool what you're doing with the apple trees, wrapping them with all that stuff.

Maybe you can show me sometime? Good summer here so far. Studying a lot and practicing and getting into shape for the new football season. Do you like sports? Don't know Fred too well, but he is a nice guy. I'll see if I can get any intel on Janelle.

JJ

P.S. I also go by JJ

William J. O'Brien

June 16th, 1983

JJ,

My grandma taught me everything about the orchards. She was super cool and I miss her all the time, although everyone said she was nuts. Saw you were practicing in the yard with your dad and he was yelling at you to work stronger. Like, what does that even mean?! I can relate. My dad is kinda like that and I also avoid him at all costs. He is obsessed with his car and that is about it. Won't let me near it to drive, even though I have my license. Loses his temper at the drop of a hat. Damn, I can't wait to get out of this town. He always talks about my clothes and appearance. But whatever, I don't really care.

And yeah, I like sports but I just watch them at this point. Been super into checking out weird records and movies from the library. Thanks for the compliments on the drawings. Do you like any particular music or movies? Gonna just sign with my initial for these notes, ya know, in case anyone finds them so people don't get the wrong idea.

T

~

June 20th, 1983

T,

    My dad is so lame. Gotta say, I was laughing so hard

Nighttime Kingdom

when you made that funny face to me when he turned his back to get on the tractor. Gotta go now. Do not know a lot of creative stuff, but think it is interesting. Be interested to learn more about records and movies. During the week I'm trapped, since I'm still grounded, but can sneak out Friday nights since my parents get so drunk in the drawing room they wouldn't notice if the damn house was on fire. Maybe we can meet up after hours on Friday to listen to some music in the orchards?

JJ

∿

June 24th, 1983

JJ,

No worries about your dad! I'm used to it. We'll just keep on avoiding each other and do our own thing. But yeah, would love to meet up sometime. I can show you some stuff about how to tend to the trees and I can bring my Walkman and we can listen to some music. Let me know.

T

∿

June 25th, 1983

T,

Let's meet up in the orchards, this Friday night. I will meet you at Aisle 2, Row 6. Tree 7 a little after sunset. Sound cool? I will wait for a half hour. If you show up, cool. If not, I'll see you around. Later.

JJ

~

When Ted arrived at their arranged spot, he saw a dark silhouette hiding behind a tree and got scared and paranoid. Shining his flashlight towards the tree, he barked in his best authoritative tone, "Who is that? I have a gun, so don't go trying to pull any shit!"

"It's just me," Jerome said, doing his best to suppress a laugh, as he emerged from behind the tree. He was wearing a Halloween mask on top of his camouflage hunting gear.

"Nice shoes," Ted pointed towards his athletic high tops, "They were your first give away."

Jerome emerged slowly from behind the tree, grasping the side of the trunk with his right hand doing a gestural spin around landing right in front of Ted, "Did I scare you?"

"You mean the mask, or this getup you're wearing?"

Jerome leaned affectionately towards him, "Perhaps I wanted to scare you."

Ted leaned in closer to his face, looking sideways with a bemused expression and putting his hand on Jerome's shoulder, "The only thing that scares me right now is having to return to the place where I just spent all day picking rotten apples to feed to the pigs... and also this getup you're wearing."

"Fair enough," Jerome remarked, as he stepped back and threw a stick he had been carrying over the tops of the orchard trees.

Nighttime Kingdom

Ted then pointed to his backpack, "You ready to party?"

Jerome stepped back and opened his arms towards the setting sun, "Yup! Been waiting all week to get out of the Hillcrest Penitentiary," then, lowering his right arm and pointing towards the direction of the Hillcrest Estate, his tone shifted, "Sure looks so nice and pretty from the from the outside, but I can tell you firsthand it does not taste like sugar and spice inside."

"Well, appearances can be deceiving," Ted said softly, putting his backpack over his shoulder and motioning with his index finger in a circular swirling pattern in the middle of his forehead. Jerome beamed, and grabbed Ted's finger, "That is what I like about you. You are not afraid to show who you are on the inside to the outside world. I think it is brave."

They both turned and meandered down the orchard aisle, beneath a sun that lingered low and lazy on the horizon. Boughs above the two boys cast long shadows in the last of that day's auburn glow as the world around them slowly succumbed to the darkness of the night. The gentle swaying of the trees and the colors of the sunset danced up ahead, making it look like they were walking into a fire whose flames were dancing westward.

When they landed at Tree 7, Ted sat down and laid out his blanket.

"This is my favorite time of the night," he said wistfully, pointing towards the night sky.

"Me too," Jerome said, sitting down next to him.

Ted had packed his bag with a few tapes to listen to, some comics, a blanket, his Walkman with an extra set of headphones, a small Thermos of vodka he stole from Ted Sr.'s stash, and a joint commandeered from the secret panel of Janelle's jewelry box. Jerome rested his head on his bent legs and looked towards the ground. Ted laid down on the blanket, interlocking his fingers behind his head.

"There are a few things I actually love about this town."

Jerome looked up from tracing a circle in the dirt with his finger, with an inquisitive look on his, "Such As?"

"You get to connect with nature here, like this. My grandma Ruthie taught me so much about listening to my senses and learning and respecting the land spirits."

"I admire that about you," Jerome said softly, looking towards Ted and meeting his eyes.

"What? That I am a freak?," Ted inquisitively responded.

"No, seriously man. You don't care what people think of you. It's very brave," Jerome was being sincere, and grabbed Ted's arm gently from the side to try and convince him of it.

"And you don't care?" Ted looked back towards Jerome, and sheepishly met his eyes.

"Of course I do! I feel like I must constantly be the best and put on a brave face. My dad doesn't care about—much less want to see—anything unique about me. Just the *Hillcrest Best,* as he says."

Ted and Jerome both slowly settled into a comfortable silence for a while then, maintaining a guarded distance from one another while laying together on the blanket. Ted turned onto his side, reached into his backpack for his Thermos, and took a sip. He tried not to wince while passing it to Ted. Then Ted pulled out the joint and lit it. He was pleased with himself that he didn't cough as he passed it to Jerome. They both laid back down and watched the twilight transition play out in the sky. As the stars started to become more pronounced, Jerome would point out different constellations and Ted would put on different tapes for music for them to listen to. Jerome picked up another stick from the ground and started balancing it on his fingertips.

Nighttime Kingdom

"You always lurk in the dark with strangers at night, Ted?"

"Nah, only during the witching hour... so I can eat and drink their blood and sacrifice them to regain my strength," he chortled, and Jerome playfully shoved his shoulder as the pair continued to watch the stars dance in and out of focus in the night sky.

Dew came down heavy in the fields the next morning. It was all over the ground, the grass, and their bodies under the blanket. As day broke, the morning light revealed how closely they were laying together. Side by side. Jerome had placed his arm over Ted's chest. When he woke up, he abruptly removed it, got up, and anxiously began walking towards Hillcrest Estate. Ted arose to the sight of him walking away and rubbed his eyes in confusion.

"Hey! If you want to do this again, hang a ribbon on the lower branch of this tree during the day and I will meet you at dusk in the same place."

"Sounds like a plan, but I gotta get home and change before anyone knows I was out for the night," Jerome yelled back over his shoulder, without slowing down.

Ted got up with a smile on his face, brushing down his shirt and pants to disperse the grass and dirt that had accumulated overnight, before walking towards the barn to change into his work clothes. Neither said anything else to the other as they walked away in different directions. It would be the beginning of the best summer either of them could remember.

Every few days, the ribbon on the apple tree would appear mysteriously before the morning orchard work crew would arrive during the work day. Freaks or jocks. Boys or men. Rich or poor. Those labels and expectations were cast aside on those nights. The apples growing alongside them in the orchards also changed and grew to their ripest potential, similarly blissfully unaware of the impending doom awaiting them at the end of the summer.

Nights together in the orchards became their secret ritual and playground. Both Ted and Jerome were given freedom from the confines of their rigid domestic spaces to be who they wanted to be. Each moment spent together, each stroll beneath those apple trees was a fleeting glimpse of the type of men they wanted to be. The expectations placed on them from their fathers, passed down from their grandfathers were asleep. It was up to them to be brave enough to break the rules and become the men they needed to be. Not everyone is brave enough to break such cycles. And some boys have no choice but to perpetuate them in order to ensure their survival. Pride can be a privilege.

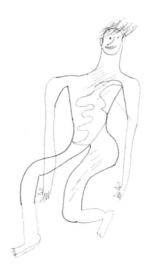

But all nights must end. The dew was wiped away each morning, burned away by the rising sun, so too was Ted and Jerome's vulnerability. Though the shackles of the roles they played during the days were mercifully lifted by the night sky,

Nighttime Kingdom

incubated beneath a blanket of stars. Listening to music, reading comics under their flashlights, getting stoned, going skinny dipping, and then sleeping together was a new and terrifying freedom that neither had experienced before. They defined the rules of this heavenly kingdom. It was their space to rule how they saw fit. A neutral space to express their authentic selves in ways they'd never been allowed. Real men were not supposed to act this way. Real men do not share headphones to listen to music and dance together. And they for sure do not giggle under a blanket together. But this kingdom had no watchers, no critics. Just the night animals who were mostly indifferent.

Some nights, Ted would talk more than Jerome. And on other nights, Jerome talked and Ted listened beside him as they looked towards the night sky. Some nights they would try on each other's clothes and laugh as they both played the opposite roles of freak versus jock for the evening. Each learned new skills and habits in this kingdom they created. For Ted, it was showing and teaching Jerome about all the different movies, books, and peculiar objects he found in the library. It allowed Jerome to drop his walls and express himself however he wanted. For Jerome, it was teaching Ted all about astronomy, tales of the different cities he'd visited with his family, and strength exercises from football training to help Ted grow stronger. Both learned that being strong and sensitive are not mutually exclusive. Neither had to choose. The definition of man can contain multitudes. Boy. Masculine. Feminine. Such bullshit did not exist in this kingdom, only what each decided for that evening at dusk.

The nights and weeks of the summer bled together and into one another as the trust between Ted and Jerome grew with each night spent together. Ted had never talked to anyone that way about how he felt about his mom, his grandmother, his dad, his dreams, or his fears before. It was at once the most exciting and terrifying chapter of his life so far.

Nature calls around the clock, and at first they were shy about peeing next to one another. As June became July, the two grew steadily more curious about what each other's bodies looked like. For Ted, it was Jerome's muscular physique. Jerome was fascinated by Ted's mere presence of chest hair. Subtle and subdued, these glances never crossed the line into affection except on the nights when it was colder and they fell asleep intertwined. This was done purely for the sake of staying warm, but there was also something else to it, something they'd find themselves denying if a hand or foot was resting in the wrong place on the other's body when they awoke.

One night, in late June when the weather was oppressively hot, Jerome suggested they run down to the pond on the other side of the property and jump in to cool off. By that point, they were naturally comfortable enough being around one another to go skinny dipping and were splashing back and forth in no time. As they got out of the water to start dressing, Ted noticed the bruises on Jerome's stomach and chest in the pale beam of his flashlight.

"What's this? Are you ok? What happened?"

Jerome quickly pulled his shirt down and pushed Ted's hand away.

"It's nothing. Like I said before, my dad is a walking time bomb. It happens occasionally. The combination of having a bad day from news about company profits, mixed with the news that I failed science for the second time in summer school, and all stirred up with a few vodka tonics and some choice words, and, well, and then you get this lovely painting," he sighed, gesturing towards the blue and yellow and purple patchwork of bruises, "Hey, you're an artist, do you like the colors used in this landscape?"

Nighttime Kingdom

"I get it, my dad does the same thing. They are all walking around like fucking time bombs with no pressure release valve except drinking. Just know, if things get bad you can always come to my house. Just throw a few stones above my window."

No further discussion about the bruises was had from then on, just a shared understanding of the repercussions and traps of the situations they found themselves in as young boys. Different? Yes, but similar. Each knew they were not the men their fathers expected them to be.

The night before Jerome was set to leave for his month-long vacation to Maine that July, he leaned over to Ted and kissed him on the cheek, "This has been fun." Ted didn't say anything. He assumed it was a joke, you know, nothing serious. Just an awkward adolescent exchange.

"You don't know everything about me, Ted Krieger."

"Meaning?"

"Sometimes not everyone is able to show who they really are inside like you can."

"I understand that. Feels like I didn't have a choice."

"We have more in common than you probably realize. Similar fathers and their expectations of what it 'means to be man.'"

"We're from different worlds,"

"You can say that again! At least you have the freedom to leave this place and be whoever you want. Meanwhile, I'm destined to be the next 'King of Hillcrest.'"

"Did you ever want to be anyone else?"

"Of course! But my father... he says I have no choice, that I have to go to a good college. Graduate. Come back. Get married to the right girl—"

Ted laughed, interrupting Ted and pulling him towards him, "Wait, the right girl?"

"Yeah they are already trying to set me up with this girl,

83

Sheila, from some fancy family in Maine. Fishing money or something. I thought we were just going on our annual summer vacation to Maine to see my grandmother, but nope, it has already been decided we 'be social' and hang with this Sheila chick and her family."

"I don't know what that is like. My father has no expectations for me. I feel like he is counting the days until I am eighteen."

"Guess the grass really is always greener on the other side. Why didn't we ever talk in school? I notice you sit by yourself in the cafeteria... always reading your art books and doing your drawings. What would the freaks or jocks say if they saw us now?"

For the month of July, Jerome is in Maine and Ted is in Hubert. The first few of the following letters Ted wrote to Jerome were never mailed, and after them are those that were. These letters are currently in Rita's baby book, under a shoebox, in Ted's closet, in St. James Place, Brooklyn:

JJ,

You are magic. You are magical. The color of your hair is midnight. Your skin is silk. Your eyes are the stars in the sky that glitter like blue opals and diamonds and I long for your touch. Even if it is only from a distance, like back when we would just lock eyes during the day. When your eyes meet mine, I feel complete. Those long nights, as we lay looking up at the stars, I was the happiest I could ever expect and have ever wanted to be with someone. One day, I will be able to touch your lips and feel your embrace. Your muscles are

Nighttime Kingdom

golden. When we are not together, I long to be. To feel your warmth next to me. To touch and brush up against you as we walk. To feel the warmth of your breath on my neck when we fall asleep. I long for your touch. I long for your eyes. My heart longs for yours each dawn when I am away, and at each sunset I ache for you.

T

~

JJ,

When we meet, the sun and moon collide. Like air and water mix. Your muscles are so hot! I cannot help staring at you when we swim together. It was so hard not to kiss your chest and neck. You are the most perfect man I have ever seen. More handsome and beautiful than Clark Kent, you are a king, and I long to be your queen and ride into the sunset together. I pretend I am sleeping some nights, so I can secretly watch you. The beauty of your breath in the night sky. I sometimes will breathe outwards and meet yours. My heart next to yours. Beating beside one another for all eternity. Beating together as we touch each other and explode. You are my man. I am your queen. We will ride into the sunset together. Anytime. Anyplace. I am here for you forever. You will have my heart forever.

T

~

JJ,

Oh, how I long for your touch! When our bodies meet it is magic. Your arms around me freezes me in delight. Your embrace is all I need. I do not need anything else. You are my food. My sustenance. My nourishment. Everything I need to live. How will I ever go without your love on this Earth? You will remain forever in my heart. I will always long for you. You are my air. My water. You are my everything.

T

Here are the actual letters that were exchanged between Ted and Jerome that July:

T,

We finally arrived in Maine. What an exhausting trip! It is really beautiful here this time of year, and the one silver lining is that my schedule is more free to do whatever I would like most of the day except during practice hours for football training and then an hour of studying for math and science. Also, Dad, Mom, and the rest of my uncles and aunts are always on their boats so I've got the house to myself most days. We eat lobster every night... which is cool, but also complicated and gross.

We constantly have people over for dinner which is great, but we also have to dress up every night and I'm not allowed to leave the table until everyone is finished. Dad is still obsessed with my talking to Sheila—my 'wife'—and he keeps putting the pressure on me to cozy up to her during cocktail hour on the terrace. I mean, sure, she is a nice enough girl but I am not

Nighttime Kingdom

attracted to her. We'll see. I hope I can figure out a way around the whole thing.

How are you? Have heard the orchards are going to have their best season ever. I think you should make apple butter for the Festival.

What I can say with absolute certainty is that my nights are not as interesting as earlier this summer. Let's try to hang out before school starts in August.

JJ

∾

JJ,

It's nice to hear from you. Work is work. Orchards are orchards. Hubert is still Hubert. Things here are the same for the most part. Janelle and I listen to records and go to the library. And that is about it. I had so much fun this summer also, and hope we can hang out more before the school year starts. I am not sure what I am going to do after graduation, but know I am getting out of this town!

Also... that skunk we saw together is still around, and me and that foreman (Mr. Wilson, dunno if you know him) have been trying to lay traps to get it since the damn thing has been stinking up the town and we can't just let it keep that up, especially not during the Festival.

William J. O'Brien

I got a few new records and tapes from the library, and a cool comic book about vampires that kill villagers in a town like Hubert. Kind of like us I guess, coming alive at night.

Hope to see you when you get back. Hit me up in August. Leave a sign on the tree when you get back.

T

Chapter 9
Foraging

Holding one's own heart does nothing to stop it from beating.

Ted exited the store in Soho and started walking South, towards Chinatown, to pick up the remaining ingredients for the apple turnovers and apple butter takeaways for Shantel's party later that day. He slowly and gently moved his hand towards his upper stomach and held it there, "I am here for you. You are going to be okay. I am not going to let anything happen to you. You are safe."

It was still early afternoon, and the sun was starting to divide the windows on the buildings in the same way he remembered in the summer of 1983. It made him smile to think of how the light would fade into the darkness with Jerome, and his heart would burn brighter than the sun as night descended upon them. The light almost seemed to glisten down and touch his heart as a sign to not shy away from the rawness that he felt during the onset of the day, back in the spice store. It was always a humbling balancing act; determining how to let oneself feel safe enough to feel what was arising, while remaining a functional adult in the world. Ted felt grateful that his professional life allowed him sufficient flexibility to do so. He knew all too well that the commotion and speed of the city afforded few such space. Most can scarcely afford to feel. They just have to make it through the day. Contending with the feelings of the past wasn't an option. But he had no choice.

Those feelings were not knocking on his door. They were kicking it down. Screaming. This required his full attention. All his efforts to forget, mold, and change himself into a different person had been temporary fixes. They always came back and manifested in different ways. They were the spirits of the people he loved coming back to pay him a visit. But it wasn't all bad. Deep down, there were things that he did love about his childhood in Hubert. The interwoven web of community in a small town breeds an intimacy that is hard, if not impossible, to recreate in the city.

Ted ruminated. It had, until he was eighteen and moved away, been necessary to hide who he really was. Shame is a trained response to avoid sincerity, and the cynicism it spawns is a poor substitute for sophistication. It was a hard negotiation. Never being allowed to truly express who he was required obscuring all of who he was—the beauty and the pain—because otherwise something might slip through. To have to constantly exist in a state of wondering if the next person he met or spoke to was okay with him existing in the world, or if deep down they thought he was wrong and needed to be fixed, was exhausting. The greatest threat to men in power is seeing others who are free from their constraints, who love and are loved, and are capable of expressing themselves unabashedly and without fear or recourse or remorse.

Was it possible to start down a path towards healing, to allow the space to address the things he had pushed down for so long? All the men in his life, at least until moving to NYC, were well trained in hiding their emotions and flattening their emotional landscapes. It was a constant balancing act to allow himself to genuinely feel vulnerable enough to address and feel the things that happened in his childhood. He lived in a world that was a constant negotiation of determining who, what, and where was a safe space. The very act of being emotionally vulnerable with another man will forever be the greatest threat to society. Wars. Violence. Aggression. All of it is upheld to avoid deeply witnessing another man.

"Ted, the only way you are going to be able to heal from the experiences of your past is by first feeling safe. Then, from that place, allowing whatever feelings need to arise to do so. Then you can talk to your inner child and make amends with what happened," Dr. Carolyn lamented. He knew and understood that. His time away from Hubert had been long enough that he could recognize that he was a strong person. And a good person, one deserving of love and a good man. It was the balancing act. A push and pull between trusting in himself that he had the strength to sit with the wounds of the past, as well as the bravery to connect those threads with the present to form a healing bond. The idea of manhood is a violent construction. A complete denial of allowing oneself to be human.

Her words rang in his ears as he shook off this constant inner dialogue that plagued him on days like this, when the past no longer seemed like it. He arrived at the intersection of Canal and strolled briskly past the produce vendors, feeling determined to temporarily focus on the task at hand. Acquire apples for the party.

Grandma Ruthie Krieger always talked about the growing of apples, and of making food out of those apples as the same as taking care of oneself or another.

As Ted walked down Crosby, towards Canal and then to the Forsyth Produce market, he was feeling in his body the wounds that wanted to be noticed and healed as a child. It always started as digestive upset, then would lead to the shaking of his nervous system. If allowed the space and trust to, as Dr. Carolyn said, "be a caring adult child to this scared, vulnerable child," these moments were rich opportunities to make amends and heal. And so he decided he was going to make apple turnovers and apple butter, and allow for the flashbacks to occur and to listen to them. To just watch and observe the scenes of the past. Jerome and his making apple butter. The events of the Festival. The aftermath. It was a humbling proposition.

Different types of apples for different types of recipes. One requiring more strength in its core, like a Granny Smith, was good for baking. More malleable and riper varieties, like a Braeburn, would delicately simmer and cook down over several hours until melded into a sultry butter.

He approached Forsyth Produce Market just when the vendors were starting to pack up for the day. "The color of apples that are required for sweetness varies from the apples that are required for strength and baking," he heard Grandma Krieger's words echoing in his head, "Do not rush your selection, the right apples will find you if they are meant to be transformed."

He stopped by a small stand, with produce from a New Jersey farm. The clerk drew their hand over their forehead to block the sun and gestured to Ted, "We have some great apples today, even though it is still early in the season."

Ted picked up a Braeburn and slowly looked at the top and

Nighttime Kingdom

bottom. He observed the shading of the multitudes of yellow, red, and brown that always reminded him of a fur coat and changed during the growing season all the way through to the harvest. Grandma Krieger's voice returned, "Look for the shading where the bands almost spread out from top to bottom from the core, and form a slight angular pattern from left to right." Ted held the apple up in the light to get a better look, carefully examining the shade and shape of the patterns. "The surface should look like the water has left tears from the morning dew, like a birthmark. That mark is the sign the land spirits have given it a blessing to be offered." He moved it closer to his nose, "If the apple is ready and willing to meet you, it will not smell too sweet. Just sweet enough that you can sense it is ready to be transformed. But not so sweet that its time has passed and will soon rot." Ted lowered the Braeburn, "I'll take everything you have left, I'm excited to go home and make some apple butter." The produce clerk handed Ted three pecks of apples, "That's the most extensive examination of apples I have ever seen." Ted smiled, "I was trained by the best."

It was just past one, and Ted had gathered all his supplies for Shantel's party as he awkwardly started descending the steps of Canal St. Subway Station to head back to Brooklyn. He swayed back and forth between the other riders with his shopping bags. He still wore a backpack that carried all his essentials. Today, he was carrying the various supplies necessary to create a ritual for Shantel and his closest friends. He kept the steps from Grandmother Krieger close to his heart. The steps for making apple butter. Though in the city it would not be made with a cauldron outside, and the steps were not perfect, but he knew in his heart she would approve of his Brooklyn apple butter. The most important aspects are embedded in the making of the recipe and how you channel and use your senses throughout the rituals. It all felt like a metaphor, going down into the bowels of the city to the subway platform. The contrasting stains of gray on the steps and walls of the subway amidst the occasional white cracked subway tile filled with stickers, tags, and scrolls marking the passing of time felt like a portrait.

Am I one of the cracked tiles? Or am I a sticker? Feels more like I am a cracked tile today, with an added layer of dirt accumulated that despite every effort can't be restored and cleaned to its original brightness. He felt as though the patina of the city was the same as himself. Weathering adds character, especially in matters of the heart and the wounds that are under the surface. Like a wonderful antique chair. The cracks and weathering over time are what make it beautiful. "Be like a tree," he heard Grandma Ruthie say, "Just let yourself sway with the wind, and trust your roots will hold you and you won't break from the storm. Don't resist Mother Nature. She is speeding things up to make us stop and notice, not to harm us."

Well, today felt speedy. Edgy. Raw. Familiar territory that paired with the lovely kaleidoscope of smells as he descended further into the bowels of the subway. Ted was a seasoned urban dweller, but today the scents felt more nostalgic as he reminisced about his first summer job at Hillcrest in Hubert.

The smells that shock your nervous system stick with you. Those acrid and acidic ones, with a strong bite. Stale urine mixed with a touch of damp wetness. Almost smelled like the hay in the barn that summer as he flashed back. A fine mixture of urine, damp wetness, and in particular the smell of hay as he stood and waited for the Brooklyn bound train to Clinton Hill.

It was all so oddly familiar. Though it had likely been produced by a human, it was reminiscent of the smell of farmyard urine and dampness as he cleaned, watered, and fed the animals in the barn that summer. The hopelessly grimy surface of the concrete floor of the subway station tickled at his nostalgia, taking him back to the stalls of the barn. No amount of water or power washing could ever remove such heavily accumulated grime.

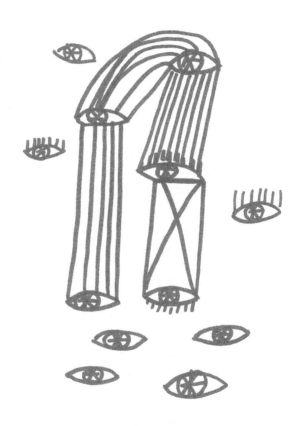

That summer had overflowed with so many mixed feelings. Bliss. Horror. Fear. Exhilaration. Heartbreak. Grief. Loss. And, most importantly, love. That balance of allowing oneself to feel safe to be oneself was hard to reconcile with the need to remain wary of the constant shadow that lingered and jeopardized any semblance of safety. The threat of being violated. All those memories for Ted were bittersweet. It was a time of connecting and falling in love for the first time, and feeling an unconditional bond with someone. It was the first time he had felt that since Grandma Krieger. It was a finding of himself, but also a total collapse and crushing sadness.

As the train groaned up to the platform, he quickly stepped inside and took a seat with his bags. It was always an expected surprise to find a seat on the train. Ted usually enjoyed people watching, but not today. He closed his eyes as the doors closed and began touching back, as Dr. Carolyn would say, "Feel your belly breathing, rising and falling. Bring your attention to that area, not just in your chest." His chest and his stomach were so connected to that summer. A wonderful opera was playing out. It was one underscored by his blissful feelings towards Jerome, though with a discordant melody of shame and secrecy that accompanied their time under the night sky.

The train clacked along, heaving and pushing between stops. Swaying back and forth and side to side in his seat, he entered the depths of the water between Manhattan and Brooklyn. He reminisced about Rita's scrapbook, which was presently sitting in his upstairs closet, and vowed that he would retrieve it once he got back and had put down all the grocery bags.

Ted emerged from the subway in Clinton Hill and walked down St James's place to his and Sam's brownstone. If there was ever a place to feel safe and secure, it was there in that home that he'd built with Sam. It was a safe space that they'd created for themselves. They set the rules for that kingdom. They dictated who was allowed in or not. It felt like it was the perfect merging of both sides of himself, *Country Ted & NYC Ted*. A sense of urban worldliness was mixed with the artifacts

Nighttime Kingdom

of the country within those walls, and it reminded him of the good parts of what home could represent. He walked up the stairs and opened the door. There were a few items of mail at the bottom in the breezeway. Maybe a few new magazines, books, or zines that would occupy his time as he read beside Sam before bed. Checking the mail was still his favorite time of the day. That was one thing that hadn't changed since he was a kid in Hubert. He still enjoyed the unexpected excitement. It was always a new thrill of discovery to escape through reading, collaging, drawing, and listening to new music.

Ted placed the grocery bags in the kitchen, to the left of the living room, and went upstairs to his bedroom to retrieve the baby book and then placed it down beside him on the couch. Sighing, he placed his hand on his chest, "You can do this. You can handle this. I am here for you, and you are safe." He opened it and experienced a mixture of joy, sadness, and curiosity while perusing and touching all the collages and drawings. He removed the unsent letters he'd written to Jerome all those years ago. They were rubber banded to the letters that Jerome had sent him. He placed them on the side, next to other mail he had brought in. He also went inside a small fold on the cover of the baby book and pulled out the last elementary school portrait of Jerome. Ted caressed that photo, and let the tears slowly form and roll down his face, "I miss you so much, and think about you at some point every day. Even today, you weirdo, I was walking down the steps to the train and smelled urine and damp hay and felt your presence meeting up with me to plan the Saturday night we would make apple butter for the Festival. Well, I'm going to make apple butter today, in your honor, and for my friend Shantel. You would really love her. I think you guys would be good friends. Miss you so much." Then he pulled the photo away from his heart, kissed it, and placed it next to the other letters and made for the kitchen to start prepping.

As he placed the apples in the sink colander to start washing, he flashed back to his old kitchen in Hubert. It was small and simple, but was perfect for making anything you wanted. There was a wide barrel sink that was used for washing and prepping. Ted now had a similarly big sink that he'd insisted on having when Sam and he moved in and remodeled the kitchen. He also recreated the same huge butcher block table that Grandpa Krieger had, which was used both to prep but also heal the townsfolk. Ted gingerly placed his hand on the surface, looking up to the ceiling, "Well, I don't do healings here Ruthie, but I sure as hell try to create your magic."

The Braeburns now washed, he started to cut and core and prep them to place in the large pot on the stove. He felt Ruthie and Jerome standing next to him, and remembered the night Jerome came over. It'd been the weekend two weeks before the Apple Butter Festival.

Chapter 10
Reunion

Mr. Wilson, the foreman of the Hillcrest barn, emerged from the barn and called Ted back from the fields. Mr. Wilson was a straight shooter, and Ted appreciated that about him. As Ted put his wheelbarrow down in between shoveling apples, Mr. Wilson placed his hand on his shoulder, "Ted, you are doing a great job here this summer and I appreciate all your help, especially now that we are starting to harvest the apples to make the first batches of cider. You need to know that not everyone in this town has an open mind. Be careful about how you express yourself, especially with Jerome Hillcrest on the fields here at night. Wouldn't want to see either of you have someone get the wrong idea... you and I both know there'd be consequences."

"I'm not sure what you mean, but I understand. I won't hang out in the orchards at night anymore with Jerome."

That single, short exchange snatched away any bliss that Ted felt and replaced it with fear and paranoia. His throat felt tight, stomach in knots, and a general feeling of guardedness descended. This fear of impending doom was deafening and the shame was heavy.

After Jerome returned from Maine, he and Ted arranged a secret rendezvous in the barn to discuss how they could still hang out with each other. They waited until dusk.

They embraced, and Jerome handed Ted a bright fluorescent pink shirt that said, *My brother went to the Cape and all I got was this stupid t-shirt*. Ted grabbed it from him and laughed, "God, I love it! It is perfect for me." Then they separated. The guardedness that was there when they first hung out had slightly returned and was dictating their body language towards one another.

"Yeah, so... I guess our summer of freedom and partying is over. At least for now. I hope we can still hang out, though. I was thinking it could be fun, like, if you were interested you could come over to my house the weekend of the 11th and we could make apple butter for the festival, and uh, then you could stay the night and we could listen to music and hang out... like, for the night. I'll prep everything."

"Sounds like a plan to me. I know we must be careful now. Wouldn't want to upset the apple cart... metaphorically," Jerome chortled, rolling his eyes towards Ted.

They both hugged and went their separate ways into the night.

As it turned out, Saturday August 11th would be the perfect time for a meetup since both Ted Sr. and Greg were going to be out of town that weekend. Ted Sr. was taking his new girlfriend for an overnight trip to Columbus for a heavy metal concert, and Greg Hillcrest was going to be in Toledo for a corporate business conference about apple farming production.

"What are you two love birds quarreling about?" Janelle

Nighttime Kingdom

exclaimed, laughing as she plunged through the screen door in her jazzercise outfit.

Ted and Jerome were coming up from the basement, struggling under the weight of Grandma Ruthie's black cauldron to get it up into the kitchen and then outside.

"Leave us alone, Janelle, we are just friends."

"Is this the 'friend' that you have been smoking all my weed you stole this summer with?"

"Yes, Janelle, you know each other already from school. This is Jerome Hillcrest."

"Nice to meet you, and thank you for sharing," Jerome croaked, shaking Janelle's hand.

"I expect to be paid, Ted, in some way."

"Well, Janelle, if you must know, Jerome and I are going to make a big batch of apple butter for the Festival and plan to win the grand prize together. So, if we do, I'll repay you."

"Wishful thinking! Well, you boys be safe and have a good time."

Ted had already prepared for Jerome's arrival by going to the orchards at dawn and scavenging for apples and placing them in the sun, on one of Grandma Ruthie's sheets, to dry.

"It is important we follow the rules. We have to set up the cauldron in a very specific way in the back, and the timing of everything is vital to get right or else it won't happen."

"Oh God! It smells like you got her crazy, too," Janelle sighed, walking into her bedroom and closing the door.

"I don't mind helping, this is super exciting for me!" Jerome said, beaming as they walked outside.

Jerome and Ted proceeded to carry the cauldron to the backyard and then placed it beside the fire pit that Grandma Krieger had used for making her annual apple butter.

"The next step is arranging the sticks on the ground in this pattern."

"Like this?"

"Yes, that's great, but we need to use this specific wood over here."

Ted and Jerome arranged the wood exactly as Ted directed.

"Okay, nice, now we just need to wait until the sun sets, in an hour or so, to get going."

"Ya know, this feels like before, but better," Jerome said softly, placing his arm on Ted's shoulder, "But we are actually going to be witches today."

"If you say so! Here, help me position the pot over the wood.

As the sun began to flirt with the horizon, Jerome and Ted sat outside together on the picnic table and caught up on all that had transpired during the month they'd been apart.

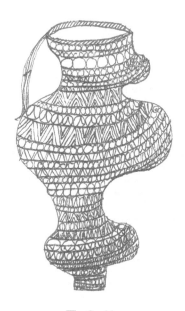

The Cauldron

"So, how was Maine?

"It was good... I missed you. My dad was really a ball of

Nighttime Kingdom

stress. I felt like I had to constantly watch what I said even more than usual, or he would have one of his episodes. He is determined that I marry that girl, Sheila."

"And how was Sheila?"

"Fine, I guess. She is not you. I wish we could run away from this town."

As the sun went down, Ted instructed Jerome to pour the apple cider that he'd brought into the cauldron, "This is the freshest you could find, right?"

"Straight from the press this morning."

"Good, that is the perfect height, now pour it into the bottom," as he said that, Ted noticed the sun had descended and it was time to light the fire. "Now we have to cut and core the apples with this particular knife."

They proceeded to cut and core and quarter the apples on the picnic table together, before placing them into the cauldron. When they were finished, they settled into their chairs, lit a joint, and started passing it back and forth while watching the fire gain momentum. The embers were catching, intercepting the crackling licks that fluttered in different shades of yellow and orange and swirled up toward the night sky from the fire pit. Ted leaned in close toward Jerome, whispering in his ear, "Now we gotta watch the fire for the rest of the night, so try not to fall asleep. We may have to get up and stir it and tell stories. Closer to the morning is the most important part. Before the break of dawn, we've got to place this spice satchel into the cauldron. Then each of us makes an offering to the land spirits and an offering to those who have passed. For this part, we must hold hands. Hope you are okay with that."

"I am willing to do whatever it takes to win this competition."

They each sat down on the folding lawn chairs and

watched the fire greedily build, and every so often one of them arose and mixed the apple butter with a wooden paddle.

"Now it is time to tell our stories to one another. They must come from the heart," Ted cooed, pinching Jerome's shoulder."

"Can I go first? I have a good story to tell."

Once upon a time, in a land far, far away there lived a small knight named Felix, in the kingdom of Onyx. It was just like the color of the night sky tonight. Deep black, but with small lines of blue that cascaded all over the expanse. He grew up thinking that the rulers of his kingdom were good, but soon learned they were evil and did evil deeds to the inhabitants. When Felix confronted the rulers about their evil deeds, they locked him in the basement of the castle. He would cry out and feel so desperately lonely while gazing out his window for someone to come and save him. One day, a cardinal came to his window who was able to talk somehow. The cardinal said he could help Felix escape if he drank a secret potion. The cardinal also said that once he drank the secret potion he would be transformed into a bird and would be set free, but would never be allowed to return to the kingdom in human form. He had only one chance to transform and escape. The bird left the potion in the window, tied with a blue ribbon. The next evening, Felix could not sleep because he was torn between choosing between staying within his comfortable life and leaving and losing everything. But he had to be set free from the prison! The day Felix awoke from his dream was the day he decided the crushing loneliness that he longed to be set free from was a greater suffering than his fear of never returning. So he drank the potion. He transformed and flew away from the prison imposed upon him by his rulers and never looked back. To this day, if you look towards the night sky and see two birds flying together you know it is Felix and a reminder to never be afraid to fly away and follow your true dreams, even if you may lose everything. To stay would have been his death.

-The end

"Will Jerome—uh, I mean Felix—ever allow himself to be himself, and get free from the kingdom?"

"Ted, it's hard to tell. Most days Felix feels powerless, and without hope. But when the bird shows up in his life, it shifts something inside him to hope that maybe there is a chance he could live in a world where he could be himself," Jerome said softly, with a distant expression and a shrug of his shoulders.

"I think that you can have everything you want and should not be afraid of the consequences. But that is not the world—and especially not the town—we live in. But I sincerely do not care anymore. I am willing to take the risk to be myself, even with the consequences. Which is why we should enter this apple butter together for the competition."

"Sounds scary, but I support that endeavor. We make a good team. Okay Ted, now it's your turn."

Before Hubert was Hubert, legend has it that it was ruled by a band of vampires that would suck on the blood of all those who tried to come and settle. Every band of travelers who tried to stop and settle in the town would notice that every night, while they slept, one of their party would disappear. To this day, they have never found the bodies of those settlers who went missing. Some say they see them roaming the orchards at night, and through the streets of this town, feasting on the apples. Every season legend says they return with the new moon, two weeks before the Festival, to be appeased or they will seek out their next victim. To prevent the vampires from returning, legend has it they started making apple butter two weeks before the

*festival. Since then, no one has gone missing in the night. Let's
hope tonight goes right for us... or we might be in trouble.*

-The end

Ted grabbed and shook Jerome from the back as he was
circling the fire, "Just kidding. Sort of. Did I scare you?"

"Did you want to scare me? The only thing that scares me
is seeing you dance around the fire telling that story, Ted
Krieger."

The pair eventually transitioned to the tent to sleep.
Though they did so on opposite sides of one another, cocooned
within the tightness of their sleeping bags. They first moved to
sleep side by side, like under the blanket back in the orchard.
As the night wore on, a hand or foot was moved alongside the
other's. But tonight there was no moving or restraint. They
both laid beside one another feeling on occasion the cold touch
of a toe that would wake the other up, mixed with the warmth
of the other's breath on their neck or back. Both were naive and
scared, but also driven by their connection to one another that
wrestled with reservations from their upbringings and the
words of their fathers and other boys in the locker room. For
just a few hours, there in the darkness under the new moon,
they connected and felt the freedom they'd savored only a
month prior in the orchard that had been their kingdom. They
both knew it was fleeting. With the school year approaching,
uncertainty loomed over the connection and threatened its
longevity. Would it be able to survive outside of this heavenly,
temporary world they'd created together? It was a world that
was never present or seen on the sidewalks of Hubert, but it
was real. It was the hearts and bodies of two boys connecting,
co-creating a place somewhere—anywhere—where their gray
guardedness could dissolve, and they could exist in a full spec-

Nighttime Kingdom

trum and without the feeling of being watched on a stage for the first indicator that what they were feeling or doing was wrong.

It existed for only a moment, as they sheltered together under the warm dark night of summer in the orchards. Glimpses were stolen, and each dazzling rendezvous was dimmed under cover of darkness and tinged with the fear of being found out. It was a scary proposition that this was what they wanted for the rest of their lives. Every night they spent together exposed the deepest parts of their souls in a way a man can only experience with another man. But they were not yet men. They existed in that malleable, vulnerable place between boyhood and manhood in which constraints and variables are yet to be cemented. It was all still to play for. There was still freedom for them, before the world demanded a different otherwise.

As they both laid there, basking in the residue of their connection, each jokingly drew pictures on the other's back and attempted to guess which scene or letter they were depicting. They each laid, with eyes closed, as the other drew a shape or word, and then the other tried to guess. And then they would switch positions and start over. It was a playful way to defuse the heat and shame that seemed to seep in after their togetherness, but the embarrassment and the speed of paranoia would eventually set in. It always did. Going back to their public personas and reassuming their guarded roles and dynamic with one another left them with few avenues of communication. Perhaps only a slight look in their eyes or other such subtle clues. They knew in their hearts what they felt was natural and right. For Ted, it was non-negotiable. For Jerome, it was a temporary fantasy. Each was meeting the other wherever they were, and each knew what they shared together was a sacred pact that no one outside it could be aware of... except perhaps by way of a dual entry in a recipe festival in a town where two boys—let alone men—had never entered together before for fear of being labeled their biggest fear. But it was symbolically important. It showed the domestic universality of love and the art it could create. And it showed that they genuinely enjoyed the company of other men, that it wasn't some shameful sexual perversion, that it went beyond the physical. That it transcended all of that.

Just before the light of dawn, Ted instructed Jerome to exit the tent with him. They both stood side by side in front of the fire, in their underwear, as Ted guided the next phase of the apple butter's conception. He threw the satchel of spices wrapped with cheesecloth into the cauldron. Next, he had them both take a handful of spice mixture. Each held the spices in one hand, while pressing together and maintaining a tight connection between the palms of their other hands for the first time. Jerome was standing on the left. Ted on the right.

"We offer these spices to the land spirits," Jerome exclaimed, as he cast the mix in his free hand up into the sky of fire. The pair watched as it ascended through the smoky rays of the dawn, and then down into the cauldron.

"We offer these spices to those who have passed before us," Ted added, before tossing his portion of the spices from his free hand into the sky.

They let their hands fall apart, looked at each other in silence for a moment, and started laughing.

"Okay! It's time to jar all this up and make some money from the festival," Ted said.

"What a bounty. I don't care what my dad says about Hillcrests entering things into the contests, I am damn proud of this work we did together and agree we should submit our entry together. Thanks, Ted. I will remember this night for the rest of my life."

Chapter 11
Inside and Outside

"Hi, is this Ted Krieger?" A hyper chipper voice peppered through the phone.

"This is him."

"This is Melissa, from Hubert Valley Realty... I'm working on selling your father, Ted Sr.'s, house."

"Right. How can I help you?"

"Well, I have some good news regarding your father's property. We have an interested buyer. A cash buyer, who wants to close as soon as possible.

"Wow, that was quick."

"Yes, it's a younger couple. They've got some serious urgency and wanna get in there as soon as possible. They were wondering if it'd be possible to close this weekend... actually, they want it to happen tomorrow."

"Wow... uh... ok."

"I know you are in NYC, and that it's gonna be inconvenient to come tomorrow, and I understand."

"No... I can come for the day. Did you tell my sister, Janelle? She might be able to come also."

"Yes, I just called her. She has a scheduling conflict, so I was calling to see if you were free. See, the buyers want to close ASAP so they can be in the house by the time the Apple Butter Festival rolls around. They want to meet tomorrow at the property so we can sign the papers and I can give them all the keys. So, can you make that work?"

"Yes, I can. I'll book the earliest flight out tomorrow, from LaGuardia to Cleveland Hopkins."

"Oh good, so let's plan on meeting at the property around noon tomorrow. Ted, I truly am sorry for the loss of your father. He was a good man, and will be sorely missed by the town of Hubert. See you tomorrow. Best."

What a weird day! I guess there is some truth that when it rains it pours, Ted thought. The doorbell then rang, Ted moved the baking trays with the apple turnovers from the oven to the countertops to cool. He had just finished sealing and jarring all the apple butter. The next step would be finishing up by putting a bow on it. Well, ribbons to be precise. He'd soon be tying blue ribbons around the tops of them and placing them out for the guests on the table settings. It was a pleasure to host, and he was looking forward to spending the night with Shantel's closest friends from the ballroom scene, as well as Sam and Felix. He let the caterers into the front entrance and directed them to the kitchen, pantry, and backdoor to get started. It had been a long day, and he needed to pace his remaining reserves of energy for the party. As Ted arranged and set the table for Shantel's party, he mentally prepared himself for the sudden shift of energy from momentary quiet to borderline chaos. The good thing was that the party was set to start earlier—around seven—so most everyone would hopefully be out the door by twelve, meaning he could get some sleep before his early flight to Cleveland. He sat down at his desk, opened his laptop, and booked the earliest flight. It was going to be at 6:oo AM. Then he'd be returning the same day, touching

Nighttime Kingdom

down back in LaGuardia by midnight. A long day? Yes. But it was better to just go and come back the same day, he reasoned. The longer he stayed, the more the past would seep into his carefully walled off psyche and erode his laboriously constructed and semi functional adult self.

What a day. What a week. What a chapter.

Ted looked down to his phone and saw a text from Felix, "Hey! So good to run into you today. I wanted to let you know I'm bringing a date to the party tonight. Did not want it to be awkward and thought you'd appreciate a heads up so you could plan accordingly."

Ted sighed and replied, "That's fine, thanks for letting me know."

He got up from the sofa and started to rearrange the table to accommodate one more person while he called Janelle. It always rang several times whenever he called her, and it wasn't until right before her voicemail cut in that she picked up.

Janelle answered, among the chaotic voices of screaming kids in the background, "So you heard, I'm assuming... surreal, right? Some urban farm to table pioneers want the house of horrors real bad. Immediate occupancy, so they can live out their apple butter provincial fantasies before the Festival next weekend."

"Right, well, I am happy. Thanks a lot for ditching me and not going to Hubert to close it out. Honestly, I do not know what to feel about the whole thing. I've got so many mixed feelings about that house and that town all tangled up in my head."

"Don't we all? That town... my God... thank God we got out of there. Seriously. Hey look, I am living my best fantasy housewife story here in the Chicago suburbs, so I just can't meet you."

"I forgive you, for now. Apparently, the new owners are obsessed with the Apple Butter Festival and are dead set on being in the house before the weekend. Isn't it surreal how that event is still going on? I guess it will forever and always be a freak magnet."

"You can say that again. Do you remember the year when all the tourists came from Australia and were sleeping in a shared tent in the town square? How did we survive?! I seriously do not know. Anyways, how have you been? I hope okay, I know the anniversary with Jerome is around this time of year."

"Thanks for asking. I don't know. To be honest, it just feels like too much. On one hand, I feel like I can't handle hosting this party but know if I am left alone, I will just be walking in circles in my head. At least this party will keep me out of trouble. My body has such strong reactions to the whole thing. I am okay though, I think my body remembers a time before my brain does. I can only fake it till I make it for so long, then I'll have to just distract myself by pretending to need something in the pantry... or, in the case of this party, constantly talking to the caterers about their personal lives. You'll never believe what I did today for Shantel's party."

"I'm afraid to ask. Please, tell me it is something legal. I don't want to know if it isn't."

"I made apple butter for the party. Grandma Ruthie's recipe. It was a good thing to do."

"Well, good for you. I for one cannot stand the smell or taste of it. I have a visceral gut response. Please give Shantel my best. God, I love her. I feel like she is the sister I never had and so wish I could be there tonight, but my kids are well adjusted and normal and I have to play like I am, too, and take them to what normal kids do like diving practice and dance competition."

"Same."

"Are you and Sam going to try to come out here soon? I

Nighttime Kingdom

hope you do get a chance to visit. I'm dying here in happy suburbia, and need my gays to break me out!"

"Definitely! I miss you guys. I wish you could come home with me tomorrow, for the closing of the haunted barn."

"Yeah, well, God... for some reason I am double booked! Darn. So sorry I can't make it. I appreciate you taking one for the team."

"Janelle..."

"Yup, baby brother?"

"Just... thank you for everything. All of it. You were the mother-dad-sister that I always needed, but never had. Just know I love you."

"You must not be okay. I love you too. Just know you are stronger than you realize. Call me when you're in Hubert if you need a voice of reason to get you back to reality. I know that place is like a time warp. Don't let the ghosts of that place psych you out!"

Ted continued to set up for the party. Once finished prepping and finalizing the table, he went upstairs, got dressed, and laid down in the bed to rest his eyes. He felt the speediness inside of him building and tried to calm down. It was not happening. Instead of sleeping, Ted ruminated. He turned the law of attraction over in his head, and how there exists some truth in it as it relates to attraction not just to things, but also people. We attract people who are similar to us. That was good through the joys, but also felt like too much in the sorrows. Another's wounds can compound and infect our own. He felt like a walking wound, and one that needed more than a Band Aid. He took his childhood scrapbook and walked upstairs to his bedroom. Ted laid down.

Sam placed a hand on Ted's shoulder and whispered, "Honey, you need to get up. Shantel and Robert are already downstairs, and the guests are starting to arrive. Felix brought this random stranger with him. Did you know he was going to?"

"Yes, he told me, I set an extra place at the table. I'll come down in a minute here, I just need to transition."

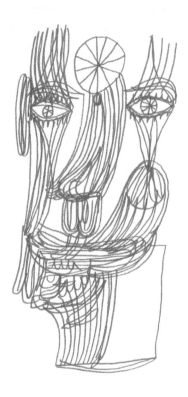

Kiss kiss. Hug. Hug. Not too close. So good to see you. Raw wound, walking around everywhere. God, I want a drink! But I can't drink tonight. It is not what I should do. Who is this random stranger with Felix? Seems nice enough. He seems happy. Shantel seems happy. They are glowing with Robert. Hope it works out. Why is the stranger putting down their glass without a coaster? Why do I care? Who am I?

Nighttime Kingdom

"Good to see you, too. Nice to see you, too. Love the earrings. Nice jacket. Love that silk."

Just keep busy. Feel like a pinball machine bouncing around this room. People seem happy. Shake. Shake. Shake. Ice clinking. Feet shuffling. Feels so hot in here! Gotta go to the bathroom great. I do not want to be stuck in there the whole night. Just do what you can. Felix's stranger looks familiar. Where have I seen him? Must just have that farm boy Midwestern gene pool, yeah that's probably it. We're probably related. Working poor white trash, dressed up in nice designer clothes. Lipstick on pigs. Can't sit still. Ants in my pants. I should say hi to Sam. He seems annoyed with me. Is he annoyed? He works so much. I wish he could get a break. Just bouncing around. My back hurts. Will just keep moving. Dance around to the other side of the couch.

"Are you enjoying the hors d'oeuvres? Need anything?"

Just hold your stomach. One foot. Then the next. Hand feels warm. Hope I'm not getting sick. Right foot left sway, ankles and toes. Shake. Shake. Shake. Olive, or no? No drinking for me tonight. More Shake. Shake Shake. I guess the stranger went to Bard. Cute shoes. Throat feels sensitive. Feels like it is on fire. Hope I'm not getting sick. Someone's hand is on my shoulder. Get it off. Feels like it is burning me. Hand is on shoulder again. Just stay for a second, make an excuse to walk out of the living room again. Pretend to check on the caterers. God, they look so

miserable and annoyed with me. This is my house. I don't care! I am allowed to cry. Oh good, everyone is starting to sit down. First course is happening. Gulp. Is that blood on the rim of my glass?

"She is doing a dance performance also upstate," Felix's stranger announced.

Uncomfortable chair. Fidgetiness. Feels like I am in Mr. S.'s class all over again here. Was he right? Am I just working poor white trash, all dressed up in a pretty little bow? I don't care. Where am I supposed to exist, exactly? Not here. Not there. Not anywhere. Necklace swings slowly on Felix's stranger's neck. Laughter across the room. Smell of smoke. Does it smell like something is burning? Make an excuse to get up. You are allowed to go to the bathroom. No one will notice. I don't like this. Why did she leave? Where was Rita and Ted Sr.? Especially Ted Sr. that day. I did love him. Jerome. Deep in my stomach and forever engraved in my heart. He was so beautiful. Like a sensitive football star. Jerome. Pure. Unadulterated. Not like me, not like now. With all these uppity queers. Smells like smoke. There were bruises everywhere. Where was social services? Why did they not intervene? I cannot imagine what it is like for queer kids there now. With the political climate. So much worse. Getting worse. Looks like blood on Felix's stranger's shirt. Oh wait... it is just a rose petal pattern.

Ted stands up from his chair and speaks to Felix and his stranger, and then raises his voice to address the rest of the guests at the table, "Do you smell smoke in here?"

Felix's stranger, "Like a cigarette?"

"No, like burning. You guys can't smell that? Like a campfire outside?"

"Nope, just smells like apple candles burning from my end."

Ted walks away from the table, "I'm gonna check on the caterers to make sure everything is okay."

Pattern of a rug on the ground. Just try to focus on your steps. Remember what Dr. Carolyn said. When you feel like you're going to fall, remember your feet and you won't. White walls with slight shadows and a picture of Sam and his mom. Flurry of tops and bottoms, black attire, walking back and forth.

"You smell smoke? I thought I smelled smoke."

"No, not in here. Happy with everything?"

"Yes. Wonderful. Having a great time. Thank you so much!"

Ted walks to the back bathroom, off of the kitchen.

Door frame. Looks like the horse barn. I did the best I could.

He glances in the mirror, doesn't like what he sees, then grabs the sink with both hands, "Get it together, Ted Krieger."

Face looks fine. Eyes fine. No blood or bruises. Good. Am I hallucinating? Jerome's chest and neck. So much bruising. Why is my hand twitching? Can't breathe. Just try to breathe. Oh God, my stomach! This better not be happening again. Just try to breathe. Sit down. Just breathe. I am here. Do not worry, I am here for you. You will be okay. No one is going to hurt you. What they did to him was terrible. I couldn't help him. It is okay to feel this. Be upset. Let it run its course.

Ted sits down on the toilet. His stomach gurgles while he absentmindedly scrolls through his phone and farts. His whole body starts shaking uncontrollably. It starts in his legs, then hands, then stomach. Like a vibrator, but on the toilet. He hates this part the most.

Oh good, it is just gas. Thank God. I can't ruin Shantel's night. Smells atrocious. Acidic. Should eat something. Try to drink some water. It's your house, they are just helping with the party.

He gets up, pulls up his pants, looks in the mirror again, and splashes his face.

Nighttime Kingdom

Who would help me if I were to fall, like Jerome? Janelle would probably help. Sam and Shantel, too, for sure. Hope Shantel is not mad at me. Feel a little dizzy here. Weight of that whole thing.

Ted hears sounds and laughter from the living room. He returns and sits down at the table. The stranger beside him kisses Felix on the cheek.

He looks like Jerome. God, I sure am losing it. Stranger danger. I love Felix... and am also jealous of him. Wish I had his financial and family support. Does he ever feel unsafe? Window is fogging up from all these people. Feels like my insides are ready to burst. Hope I am not acting weird for Shantel's party. Gotta just keep my head down and keep to myself. Hide in the bathroom. What is that girl doing outside, in our front garden? Better clean it up afterwards... should I go outside and make sure? Will check later, I need to try to just sit down for now. What a nice spread. Can't believe I made apple turnovers and apple butter. This chair is burning my ass. Cannot sit still. Feels like a knife in my right cheek. He had such a nice chest and ass. God, he would probably have become a circuit queen. Would we have still been friends, or even have stayed together if it didn't happen? Why are there no condiments on the table? That's a great excuse for me to get up again. Go to the pantry.

Ted gets up abruptly from the table, again unnoticed, and says to Felix and the stranger, "So sorry we do not have the condiments out for the main entrée, I'll go grab them now."

He walks to the pantry and peers around the shelves.

~

Smells like rot in here. Or is it just me?

~

Ted rummages around, eventually finding the condiments and placing them on the kitchen counter.

~

Does Sam know this gingerbread has been here since last Christmas? Does he still love me? Of course... I hope. I love him, and I need to tell him about what happened with Jerome. So scared. But it needs to happen. The longer I wait, the more upset he will be that I kept it secret from him.

~

Ted returns to the dining table, proclaiming loudly over the table of guests, "Sam, did you know you have a gingerbread house back there?"

Everyone turns their heads to face him, looking confused.

Sam responds, "Wait, what are you talking about? What happened to the condiments, dear?"

Ted sits back down. Felix and the stranger continue their discussion of the show at the museum and the performance, agreeing that the tensions from the old collection and the new voices colliding in between the sculptures is an amazing critique of the institution, but in a good way.

When was the last time I went to a museum? Food looks nice. Is that blood in my mouth? No, just some wine. Thank God. Weather was at least nice today. Hope Shantel is happy. She looks happy. God, this day. What a day! It will never end. All I want is to escape this body and the God forsaken heat of this table. So many pings from the moving of the forks and knives. Too loud, too much noise. Going to put on the mix I made to distract myself. Such a nice mix. Soothing. Romantic. Are Sam and I romantic anymore? I think we are... at least most days. He is so tolerant of me and my stuff. I do not know if I would be so tolerant. God, what is that itch on my neck? I cannot deal with another rash. It's probably just dry skin. It is so hot in this room. Need to see if the air conditioning is on. That's a nice color on Shantel's shirt. Is it a forest green, or just a regular dark green? Looks like the color of the tree outside Jerome's bedroom. God, he never knew how I felt. I stalked him that whole summer. What is the difference between a stalker and a lover? They seem pretty similar on the surface. I feel like all gay men are stalkers. Vampires. God, this day. Jerome. All of it. The day of the anniversary. It just keeps dragging on, hour by hour. I feel like I am on speed, but with no caffeine. Should I drink some water? Have I had any water at all today? I can't remember. Did I ever drink water as a child? I can't remember. Rita and Ted Sr.— Mommy and Daddy—were so self-involved. Why do people have children? Well, they birthed me. I didn't ask for that. Now I have to deal with existence. Despite that, dying outweighs the other fears. Where was he? Where was my father when all of this stuff was going on? Where the fuck was he? I was just a kid...

well, almost an adult, but still. I see these kids on the subway who are seventeen and realize they are still children. I realize I was still a child. Where was everyone? Why didn't they see and help us? Where was my dad? Probably drunk. Thanks Rita. Thanks for nothing. You just do you. Go ahead. Abandon me for your boyfriend. God, I am so mad.

Ted turns to the stranger and Felix, "Why would you say that about the show at the museum? The way I see it, it represents an intersection of painting and craft. Is not craft a form of art?"

What is my problem? Felix's stranger is a nice person. I need to get up from this table. Why does it feel so hot? Is the air conditioning on? Am I jealous that he also comes from money? Is that it? Is that why I was always attracted to Jerome, from the very beginning. Did I secretly want to be what I hate? I should probably check in with work. They probably have not even noticed I am not there. I am trying. I should keep going to therapy. I think it is working. How is sitting with this shit actually productive? I want a drink. I can't ruin Shantel's party. Is it normal to hate and love all of your friends at the same time? Is that what chosen family is? I do love these people... I just want out of this godforsaken chair. It feels like I am sitting on nails. Is a prerequisite of good design that it be uncomfortable? Did I ever have a chair I sat on and ate a meal on as kid? I feel like we always ate in front of the TV. I should try to eat something. Feels like I could barf at any moment. Skin feels so sensitive and raw. Where the fuck was Rita? Seriously... she can't return her kid's phone calls? Seriously, what gives, Rita?

Nighttime Kingdom

❧

Ted speaks louder again, from the other end of the table over the guests laughing and talking, "Sam! Is the air conditioning on? I'm gonna check and see, feels so hot in here to me."

Ted walks over to the switch on the wall, verifies it is on, and returns to his seat.

❧

So hot in here. I better not have to go to the bathroom again. Do not ruin this night for Shantel! Does everyone notice how uncomfortable and fidgety I am? Wish I could fall into Sam's arms. My substitute parent. Dad. Mom. Everything. What would I do without him? He seems annoyed with me. Shantel's boyfriend is so nice, I hope it works out for them. She deserves the best. He seems privileged, like Felix and the stranger. I wonder if they all went to the same boarding school? Probably. God, can you imagine if they actually knew Jerome Hillcrest? I can't deal with that. I feel like I am a fraud, standing here like this and walking around and talking to the caterers like this is my world. They see right through my bullshit. Well, they are getting paid. I know. I get it. I have been on that side. I will always be on that side. Why is Shantel's boyfriend leaning on the chair like that? Should I say something? No, don't say anything. Let it go. Why can't I let it go? It must be nice to be able to just be. I do not know at all what that feels like. This godforsaken weekend. It will haunt me forever. I wish he was here. Will Sam be upset with me when he finds out about Jerome and the past? Probably not. He seems annoyed with me already. I keep fidgeting and walking around the table and asking if anyone needs anything. Do you think Jerome felt this way before it happened? Who knows. My body feels so confused, like it does not know if it should run outside screaming or go to the bathroom or go to bed. Oh good, the main course. Going to sit down at my seat again. Looks delicious. Glad we got a caterer. I could never have made this. She deserves it. We deserve it. Must try to eat. Tastes good. I need to eat more. Got to remember to breathe and listen to my inner child. Well, my inner child wants to get the fuck out of here... and go to Tahiti?

Ted blurts out to the table, "Tahiti! Guess I am going to Tahiti!"

The stranger sitting next to him looks confused, and says, "What did you say, Ted, about Tahiti? I have never been there, but Bali I heard is incredible. The flight is the worst part. We never travel as much these days, because of the pandemic."

"Oh, nothing, I just need a vacation... maybe Tahiti?"

The vegetables are bruised. Am I really bruised? They look like they are supposed to be that way. Bruises. God, remember his bruises? They were bad. It was like looking at a haunted house. I still love him. Is asparagus supposed to be burnt? Should I say something? I mean, we are paying for this shit. It isn't some cheap takeout meal. Yes, I think they are supposed to be burnt. Still tastes good. Never had this before. Did I even eat vegetables as a child? Apples. Lots of lunch meat. Canned goods. Beans.. yeah, I know what that looks like. Bruising. Bruises. I am going to report the chef for doing this. Tastes pretty good.

"How do you like the food so far? Are you guys having a nice time?" Ted beams, while leaning over to Felix and the stranger.

"So delicious! This asparagus, I love how it was seared. A truly beautiful meal and night so far, thanks for letting me come with Felix. Appreciate it. You and Sam have such a lovely home."

Dessert course. Thank God. It is almost over. The turnovers I made. They look okay. Good enough to eat. I tried. Good thing they're also served with a side of chocolate. Hilarious that Ruthie thought sugar was the devil. Well, if she talked to the exercise fanatics in Chelsea they would agree. Cannot believe that queen on the beach in Miami saying he felt fat from eating mango slices while on vacation! Well, I have eaten many different types of mango slices. Can't seem to slow down. It is okay. Dr. Carolyn says to just let the emotions ride themselves out. The shaky tenderness is okay. And no one sees what you are feeling inside and, if you need, you can always go to a bathroom stall and breathe it out. I can't go to the bathroom again. This is nice though. Chocolate is always soothing. Did we even have chocolate in Hubert? We must have. I never remember bringing cupcakes to school for my birthday. The things you do and do not notice as a child. That snack lady. Always glaring down at me. Well, look at me now, Ms. Snack lady! Here I am, in my Brooklyn brownstone, eating high end dessert!

"Ted. Ted. Ted! Earth to Ted!" Sam yells across the table.

"Yes. Yes. Sorry," Ted looks up to the rest of the table, blushing with embarrassment.

"Do you want to share about the apple butter you made for our guests tonight?"

"Yes I apologize, I was just enjoying this dessert so much I was totally immersed!"

As Ted slowly gets up from his chair, he notices he spilled a drop of wine on his shirt. He brushes it away with his napkin and looks out over the table.

"I first want to toast to Shantel and her beautiful fiancée, Rob. I have never seen Shantel happier, and wish you a long wonderful meaningful life, cheers!"

Clinking of glasses echoes and the sounds of laughter ripples throughout the table and room. There's an exchange of eyes on opposite sides of the table. More glasses clinking. Ted places a hand on the table.

"So, today I decided to make apple butter... some of you may not know, but I grew up in a town that is... well... not really a town. But yes, technically it's a small town. And it is a town that was obsessed with and existed because of apples. My grandma, Ruthie, lived there... she was an incredible person," Ted pauses, sighs, and looks toward the ceiling. "She was a mother to me, just as Shantel has been. Today, I remade her recipe... to the best of my abilities. I hope you can enjoy this symbol and gesture of how I view Shantel. Warm. Sweet. Spicy, with a big heart of love to all of us. So, please enjoy it in the forthcoming winter months with someone you love... cheers!"

Felix's stranger piped up, "My grandma made apple butter also."

"Oh, really? That's amazing. Where are you from?"

"A small no name town in Indiana."

Ted winks, "Most of us are from small no name towns. Thanks for coming, it was great to meet you and I hope to see you soon with Felix. Let's meet up for brunch soon!"

Nighttime Kingdom

Guests start to disperse from the table and mingle towards the front of the breezeway.

∼

Good I can just focus on cleaning now, and avoid everyone.

∼

Ted begins stacking the dishes and moving the food into the garbage and organizing the leftovers.

"Hey, are you okay? I can tell you have the feels today," Shantel says softly, grabbing Ted's arm and pulling him towards them.

"Yeah... well, it's the anniversary. *The* anniversary."

"Oh, I see," she whispers, and hugs Ted. "You are strong, and you are also a mother to me. An inner light. Never forget that."

"Thank you. Hey, I hope I didn't distract from your party."

"Not at all. Felt it in my body. Same feeling. Different memories. Pain. Trauma. But same feeling. Be nice to yourself."

"I am trying to be proud of myself and proud that I didn't drink as much tonight as I would normally. If I had, well, then this party would have gotten messier much quicker."

Rob comes from behind Shantel and kisses her neck while wrapping his arms around her stomach, "I see my *king* has returned."

"Thanks to you, to Sam, and to everyone for tonight. It was one of the happiest of my life!"

"Of course," Ted exclaims, then hugs both Rob and Shantel awkwardly.

Ted walks Shantel and Rob to the breezeway of the brownstone, where Sam has already been having a lively and jolly departing discussion with the guests as they shuffle out. He kisses and hugs both Shantel and Rob.

Ted returns to the living room and starts cleaning up the remaining dishes and places them in the dishwasher. He turns it on and walks up the stairs. Sam is in the bathroom, flossing and brushing his teeth in the mirror.

"You okay? You seemed off today and tonight."

"Yeah I am. Just a long day. I need to talk with you about something and am so worried you will be upset," Ted meets Sam's eyes in the bathroom mirror, mid-flossing. Sam stops and replies to Ted, "Is this about the baby book on the bed? I just peeked. Hope you are not mad. I just have never seen any baby photos of you."

"Oh no, I am not mad about that. It is a book from my child-hood, from after Rita left. I filled it with all my dreams and fantasies, back when I was alone in my room.

"Looks pretty amazing."

"Thanks... so, uh, well, Sam... I need to be honest with you... I haven't told you about the first person I fell in love with, back when I was in Hubert. It is one of the reasons why I went into therapy. My junior year of high school, I started working in the orchards and ended up meeting and falling in love with Jerome Hillcrest, the only son of the owners. We had an amazing summer. He was my first love. But he also died tragi-cally that summer. And a part of me died with him. I blame myself for what happened, but I was so young. And he was so young and now I can see that his pain and the circumstances were out of my control. I have carried this shame and guilt around my neck for years. I never told you about it because I think a part of me was worried you would judge me... or leave me when you found out the first person that I fell in love with and slept with died tragically a few days later. It's so dark, I

128

Nighttime Kingdom

know, but... " Ted trails off, looking down sheepishly to avoid Sam's gaze.

Sam pulls Ted's chin up softly so that their eyes meet, and whispers, "When you are ready to talk about it and tell me more about Jerome, I am ready. I am proud you told me. Some of the things that happened to us as children are hard to understand until much later. As kids—and even as adults—we do not have the skills. All that shit just accumulates and manifests in our bodies. No matter what you want me to know, just know I love you. Let's try to get to some rest. You've got an early start to go back to Hubert tomorrow."

Chapter 12
The Hubert Apple Butter Festival of 1983

Friday, September 20, 1983

The light of the full moon cast a shadow over the huddled figures gathered in the town square. The candles were lit one by one. The mayor of the town of Hubert was the first to take his candlestick and light it from the burning fire. He pulled the candle away and gestured with his free hand to draw a star formation above his shoulder in the air towards the sky. The rows of school aged children were already in formation behind him. There were double rows of children as far as the eye could see. Beyond the children were the city elders, the council, and then, in descending chronological order, the remaining citizens of Hubert. They each lit their own candle one by one, and then turned and bowed and shared the collective flame until the entire village of Hubert was all illuminated. It was the official start of the 1983 Hubert Apple Butter Festival.

As the procession started around the town square, each school aged child moved slowly forward, clockwise around the square three times. It was playing out just as they had practiced

Nighttime Kingdom

for the last four weeks in summer camp, in front of the library. Everyone was either wearing a *prince* or *princess, or king or queen* handmade paper crown. Some had been passed down in families through the generations, and others were just made from cardboard and decorated with a personalized touch. A family insignia. Illustrations of different types of apples. Extra string. Tin foil. Glitter. Some had custom made designs of the orchards that were sewn, stitched, or embroidered from the sewing groups from years gone by. It was a representation of past, present, and future. A bounty. The harvest of the season. Hope for the future.

As the progression started to build momentum around the town square, the townspeople who were still tasked with finishing up the remaining elements of preparation for the festival joined, and lit their candles. They were all there. Or at least the people who were currently living in Hubert were. Everyone from the town had come together for this. The sick were being pushed in wheelchairs and the more virile were dancing around as the progression slowed down and sped up. The outcasts. Freaks and jocks. Orchard and cannery workers. Teachers. Librarians. Mechanics. Everyone. Especially the corporate reps from the Hillcrest Orchard. It was the most important work weekend of the entire year for the entire town.

In unison, some in tune and others way off, they started to sing the anthem of Hubert as they crossed the threshold into the gates of the Apple Butter festival,

To sacrifice oneself for the sake of another... is the ultimate service to community... together in spirit we rise... to work together for the harvest... we are proud of our labor... a labor of service with one another... the core of us like our apples... defines the spirit of grace and hope...

As the crowds continued to swell, the chorus steadily increased. Birds left their nests. The wind picked up and started to tip and blow out their candles. All in unison, step by step, quiet and then at times more spirited. Then they peeled off from the square and walked down Middleton Rd, passing by the Krieger horse barn house, past the Hillcrest Estate, and then ending in the first rows of the apple fields.

We will grow and work together, for a united front, as one town and to our nation...

Everyone blew out their candles and the mayor exclaimed, "Let the festivities begin!" As the crowds lingered, so did the scent of apple cinnamon that permeated the air from all directions. That sweetness was inescapable. And it was a false sweetness that embedded itself in fabrics, and if you were working a food station your hair and clothes would hum of it for the entire weekend. The smell of sweetness embedded with desperation lingered everywhere. Things had to go well for the next three days. The town's livelihood depended upon it. It was as if the entire town of Hubert was one large play on opening night. The actors taking their positions. Smiles. Friendliness. Cues everyone. Remember our values. Small American town. Give them what they drove an hour to the country for. A performance of pastoral quaintness. Remind them of good memories. Listen to their stories. Promote the town. Sell the products. It was all a performance.

It was the start of another round. The beginning of the official harvest season. It was the most important weekend of the year for Hubert. It was her sustenance. Every year, the same families and apple enthusiasts from the tristate area would descend upon the town for three days. Ted and Jerome had not

Nighttime Kingdom

seen one another, apart from at a distance, since the night they'd made apple butter together two weeks prior. He always connected with the opening ceremonies for the festival. The singing procession and the offering in the orchard left a resonance with him and his memories of Grandma Krieger. She sure got into the swing of things, and would—until he refused when he got a little older—dress him up like a *king* or *queen* of the orchard to make an offering to the land spirits. Who were the land spirits, exactly? They seemed made up, but it was all rooted apparently in old Norse mythology. Ted went for the procession every year. He was hoping to see Jerome, and saw a light on in the Hillcrest Estate when they walked by. It was assumed he had to entertain the out-of-town celebrities or politicians that had arrived for the weekend to judge the apple butter competition.

The preparation for the town occupied the two weeks before all the guests arrived, and everyone had an essential part in it. From the school kids to the senior citizens at the retirement home, all worked towards the festival. It was really a year-round effort, but those two weeks were a flurry of activity. Some oversaw preparing the tags and buttons for the registrations. Others oversaw the logistics of moving all the furniture and tables that had been in deep storage all around the town to the town square. As the weeks and days before the festival drew closer, so did the transformation of the town. All the picket fences, sign poles, and spaces had blue ribbons attached, with apple paper designs interspersed between that had the new year advertised. There was a competition held to determine the design used each year. The winner of this year was a classmate of Ted and Jerome's, Lisa Stansfield, who came up with the slogan, 'The sweetness of the apple is the same as the sweetness of community.' She got to see it printed on thousands of flyers, cups, signs, and any possible surface that could serve as a potential advertisement for Hubert.

Most years, Ted was asked to help move the folding tables and help set up the tents in the main square. This year, because he was actively working in the Hillcrest Orchards, his job was to assist in the actual harvesting of apples to be used for apple cider, applesauce, and—most importantly—apple butter. It was imperative that there be an ample supply available for the tidal wave of visitors that would soon descend.

The whole main square of Hubert was shut down to traffic, which was always a headache for the owners of the homes leading up to the square but would also make extra money for them by offering their driveways and lawns for parking. It was part of the charm that the people coming from the city, and sometimes believe it or not all the way from Australia or India, loved. It was the quintessential small American town experience. The smell of apple cider donuts, warm apple cider in their mugs, and the ability to take home apple butter to be reminded of the charm of it all.

The procession was on Thursday night. It would start the Festival. Friday was the official opening, with the townsfolk starting to make huge batches of apple butter in the town square and they'd allow visitors to come and turn the big ladles as part of the entertainment. There were cooking demonstrations, hayrides, apple pancake breakfasts, and of course the apple butter contest was judged. The best in show category had a prize of $5,000, first prize was $2,500, second was $1,000, and third was $500. The honorable mentions received a ribbon, but that was it.

Friday morning was the time slot to enter the competition. At least half of the panel of judges always consisted of citizens of the town of Hubert, and the other half was a mix of celebri-

Nighttime Kingdom

ties, local radio DJs, and usually politicians running for office. The judging was always done privately. The only qualifications for entry into the competition were that you had to have made a form of actual apple butter and jarred it into containers. For the competition, you submitted two jars. One was never opened, and just examined by the outside for its form, substance, and texture as they held it up to the light. The other jar was opened and sampled by the judges. Each would take two spoonfuls. One was a direct taste, and the second was used on top of a vessel of their choice, usually a form of bread.

When Ted approached the table, he greeted Mr. S and placed his two jars down on the surface, along with his entry form.

"I am entering the competition this year, Mr. S., and I'm determined to win."

"I see, that's great, Ted. We have a lot of good competition this year. I hope you get placed. I see here that you and Jerome Hillcrest are submitting as a team entry. Is this correct?"

"Yes, it is. We made it together and we make a good team... turns out detention may form lasting friendships!"

Ted left without another word and walked away from the table. It was the first public statement of his 'friendship' with Jerome, and until that point he had not worried or been too concerned about it. Yes, it could look weird for two grown teenage boys to have made apple butter together, but who cares? It was for the money.

For the rest of the first day, he kept searching for Jerome in the orchard fields and town square to let him know that the entry was official. He didn't find him. Janelle mentioned not to worry, and that he probably was just immersed in Hillcrest Corporate hell and wrangling the pressure of the profits for that season. She mentioned that she'd heard from Ted Sr. that

135

there was a potential bankruptcy issue looming if the Festival and this harvest season did not produce record profit and that layoffs would happen as a result.

Ted felt in the pit of his stomach that something was off, but couldn't decipher what it could be. There were so many variables that could determine his absence, including those concerning Ted, but he could not speak with him directly in public so had to bide his time and distract himself by walking the festival. So, he decided to follow Janelle around to completely distract himself by engaging in her social drama that revolved around who was chosen to be selected for the Junior Apple Butter Festival. After that, he found himself engaging in Janelle's own personal dramas of who was chosen for Junior Apple Butter King and Queen... thought this was of no concern or interest to Ted.

It is a strange feeling to long for someone but to also suffer in silence. To feel a sense of desire and craving that is quelled by the fear of discovery. You walk around, remaining behind others in power who parade their lives in front of yours and are unaware of the privilege they wield. You suffer in silence behind them. It is learned by watching. When to lock eyes. When to avoid contact. When to move. Normal days for some, but for Ted this was the imposition he found himself in while both longing for Jerome but also being acutely aware of the fear and consequences of being discovered.

There are many different types of longing, just as there are many different types of touch. The longing for the beginning of a day. The desire for the day to end. The longing for an embrace, or to be noticed by a stranger on the street. The desire for something sweet to eat. The desire to want to be seen and held close by a romantic partner. A desire to see the pleasure of revenge on someone. Through all the years of growing up, Ted

Nighttime Kingdom

had only really known one type of affection or desire. Now he did not know how to contend with longing and feeling that for someone in a place that was a prison for his heart.

Ted stood and watched a carnival ride take a group of kids upwards and then shift them down abruptly from side to side. The kids screamed in delight and terror. He thought to himself that he felt the same uncomfortable maelstrom of emotions. It was unavoidable. His mind tumbled down and around, evaluating all of the different reasons why he had not seen Jerome yet after speaking to each other briefly by the apple tree and arranging that they would still pass notes to one another. It was assumed that they would both be very busy and would see each other in public for the Festival to be able hang out, even if it was under the constant and oppressive eyes of the town. He decided to leave a simple note for Jerome under the apple tree. The note left for Jerome that evening read:

JJ:

I entered our apple butter in the contest today. Have not seen you around. Hope all is okay. Just throw a few stones outside my bedroom window if you want to chat.

T

He tied the blue ribbon to the tree marked Aisle 2 Row 6 Tree 7, and went home for the night to sleep. It was a restless slumber. He was too desperately desiring to hear a knock at his window to fully switch off. It did not occur. His stomach was in knots. The reality that he was in trouble—or about to be in trouble—for the things he'd done with Jerome that summer was setting in. Had Jerome confessed to what Ted and he had done?

Was he in trouble also? That night, Ted had a nightmare. The narrator of the dream stared down from above him, and at random intervals snakes would be released into Ted's home through the vents and slithered through the small cracks and spaces and it was up to Ted and the other person in the room to find the snakes, befriend them, and remove them.

The whole premise of the dream was powerlessness and fear. One snake was yellow and black and had positioned himself under the small space between the coils and mattress of Ted's bed frame. It was venomous, but also quiet, and was waiting to pounce upon its next victim. It was hard to deter-

Nighttime Kingdom

mine if the snake was his enemy or his ally. At one point, the narrator of the dream spoke to Ted, "Ya know, the snakes are very friendly... you just have to let your guard down and not be afraid to befriend them." He also saw there was another figure in the room, in the corner, shrouded in darkness, who was shivering and afraid to come forward. Ted gestured to it, "Don't be afraid, I am not going to hurt you. We must work on this together to make it out of this house alive."

Saturday, September 21, 1983

Ted woke abruptly to his alarm going off in his bedroom. He slowly emerged from the cove in the back of his closet, rubbing his eyes and peering out to see the time. It was still early in the morning, before the resurgence of crowds. It was the second day of the Apple Butter Festival in Hubert. That morning, the food tent (the largest tent structure within the Festival) was hosting the annual pancake breakfast for everyone in town. It was the single most important temporary tent structure that was raised in preparation for the festival. It housed all the cooks and stations that were to prepare food and drinks from the apples that were also manufactured as products for sale by the Hillcrest Orchard Corporation. It was a living, breathing artery of advertisement for the entire town. If Ted was going to run into Jerome, it would most likely be there. Pretty much everyone who lived and worked in Hubert went there first, before the visitors arrived for day two. Ted still felt a restlessness clawing away inside of him. Deep down, Ted was coaching and convincing himself that he was just paranoid since it had not been that long since the last time he'd seen Jerome. Everyone in the town was required to participate in some way leading up to the Festival, so it was common to not see people until everything ended. Additionally, It was known that the Hillcrest family hosted a special VIP reception at the estate on Friday evening. So, even though Ted felt a sense of urgency about the fact that he had entered their apple butter together for the competition the previous day, it did not necessarily mean anything more. Kids with their mothers did team entries. Grandmothers entered with their grandsons. It just so happened two teenage boys had entered together, and the way that Ted discussed it with Mr. S. the previous day was under the guise of trying to make some money. Good old capitalism to the rescue. Ted just coincidentally knew how to make his Grandma Ruthie's recipe that had won Best in Show continuously for over a decade. It was not weird at all. But all that self-talk did not help him feel more confident as he paced around the town square and throughout the festival. Everywhere he went, he felt paranoid that every passing gesture on the sidewalk was connected to the judgmental eyes of the town raining down on him. They knew.

The town of Hubert looked completely different on the Saturday morning of the Festival. It was a living, glowing testament to the entire year of preparations that would bloom for just three days. An entire year's worth of work for only three days. The town square had been transformed into several temporary tent structures that were all decorated on the sides with blue ribbons and interlaced with apple paper stencils that each bore the new slogan. In the direct center of the square was the main entrance, which still had the original log cabin structure straight ahead and also five large cauldrons. The cauldrons in front were the official town batches of apple butter that were simmered during the festival. As the tourists rolled through the main festival entrance, they could stop for the quintessential tourist photo opportunity of stirring the batches in progress

Nighttime Kingdom

with a large wooden paddle. As you went deeper into the festival grounds, there was a maze of interconnected temporary tent buildings that were constructed for the weekend. Most were antique wooden structures, so as you stepped across the floorboards they'd creak. There were no straight lines in the carpentry of these structures, and the joinery had been dismantled and reassembled annually for decades, so a chorus of small noises was produced as the structures heaved under the weight of the crowds of tourists making their way from tent to tent.

The top portions of the temporary structures were hewn from canvas that seemed to date back to the founding of the town, with patches stitched on patches of all different fabrics over the years that'd been donated by the generations of families who worked in the orchards. An annual sew-in happened during the fall and winter months in the library, where people would bring their old clothes and cut them up and then sit and repair any holes that'd formed. Looking up, it added to the quaint feel of the town, and the tourists loved taking photos standing beside the patchwork tapestries that stretched upwards into the late summer sky. The festival was also always hosted and ended before the official start of the first day of school so as to ensure everyone in town was able to work continuously to ensure it was a success. The tent structures were a symbol of community also, where different generations would pass through the tents together pointing up to an item of clothing that was still present from their great-grandparents or grandparents and was still holding the town together. The canvas patchwork of the tent structures was held up by the same antique pole it'd always been. Much like a barn, raising the tents for the festival was a community job requiring the strongest thirty or forty people from the town of Hubert to heave and will the largest pole into place. One step up and everyone around the town square would hear the click, click, clicking of the pulley system as everyone struggled to get the canvas to the highest points.

Ted looked up to the ceiling of the food tent as he first entered and tried to see patches of clothing which he'd helped repair it with alongside Grandma Ruthie over the years. Perhaps a momentary pause to reflect on this would uplift his sense of dread and paranoia he thought, as he entered the biggest tent structure and crossed the threshold of the official entrance of the Festival. It was deemed multipurpose, but was used for the making and serving of food to one side with the other side displaying the corporate versions of the food that were being actively made and distributed by the Hillcrest Orchards Corporation. Looking around the tent, he observed a distinct silence and exhaustion emanating from the citizens of Hubert who were silently eating. They were all performing that weekend, and were feeling the effects of the second day of the festival. Ted walked over to the food line and grabbed a plate and some plastic silverware, then began going through the buffet to grab apple pancakes, an apple cider donut, and lastly a small paper cup of juice at the end of the table. As he turned around, avoiding all eye contact, he noticed Janelle was sitting at a table towards the back of the tent. He started walking over and took a seat at the picnic table next to her. She had a fresh plate of pancakes, sausage, and a small paper cup of juice next to her also.

"Well, here we are... another festival underway! I wonder who all these people that magically show up here for 48 hours and then leave are?" He said, nudging Janelle with his elbow.

"I have no idea... and am totally exhausted. Mr S. asked me to coordinate the pony rides this afternoon and, frankly, I do not know if I have the capacity. What is your required day job?

Nighttime Kingdom

"I'm supposed to sell tickets for the apple dunking station for the rest of the morning, and then plan on going over to the awards tent to see who was given the awards this year."

"Did you enter the apple butter you and Jerome made? I still want my money back, you know," she pouted, rubbing her fingers together in the universal gesture for 'pay up, buck-o.'

Ted laughed, almost spitting out his juice, "I know! I know... okay. I haven't seen Jerome around at all and am assuming he is in a different social atmosphere because of Hillcrest Orchards corporate. You haven't seen him around, have you?"

"No but I am usually completely self-involved and in my head, so he could have walked past right by me and I wouldn't have noticed."

"Understood. If you see him, can you tell him I am going to be in the awards tent to see what happens with our entry?"

"No problem. Well, I'm off to give pony rides to the finest of America."

It was a nice distraction to talk with Janelle, Ted thought, as he finished his pancakes and got up and moved toward the dunk tank ticket booth. A local disk jockey for FM 93.5 was inside and was navigating how to sell tickets. He considered he was probably fine and just busy with stuff his dad was making him do and that he'd most likely see him later, at the prize booth and award ceremony.

As the hours flittered by selling tickets, Ted sat in a daze just watching the throngs of visitors passing in their ugly flip flops, atrocious jean shorts, and in some cases matching outfits. He looked upwards towards the clock on the telephone pole and saw it was 1:50 and so decided to start heading over to the awards tent to see the results. For the most part, the awards ceremony was uneventful. There was just a brief announcement from Greg Hillcrest—Jerome's father, and president of Hillcrest Orchards—in which he thanked everyone and then proceeded to promote the brand. He then moved on to the announcements and prize ceremony, which was done by the events coordinator of the competition. This year, that person was Mr. S..

Ted walked slowly into the award tent and surveyed the somewhat full crowd. It mostly consisted of grandmothers, a few ambitious cooks, and a few urban-to-farm pioneer cooks surveying the cage presentation of entries. He did not see Jerome at all, so meandered to the side of the tent and leaned on the opposite wall to the stage. All the entries for the competition were presented elegantly on one side of the room. There was a podium structure that went upwards, with those garnering the top prizes at the top row. There were probably a hundred jars on display, in various roles and categories. This way, before the official ceremony started, you could see if you'd won a prize if your entry jar was positioned towards the top and they designated it a prize winner with a ribbon. Best in Show was at the top row, first from the left, and from there the prizes were displayed in descending order. It was a beautiful display of all the category winners. Looking left to right, the rows were arranged in order of, *Best in Show, First Prize, Second Prize,* and *Honorable Mentions.*

Summoning all his courage and apprehension, Ted edged slowly back and forth in an effort to squeeze in between the spectators who were examining all the entries in front of the display case. Because of issues with crowd control and theft in the past, they'd constructed a screen door window barrier between the spectators and winners. It almost looked like the competition jars were wild animals that needed to be protected. It was just a precaution, though, to prevent any

Nighttime Kingdom

tourists seeing the top prizes and snatching one and taking it back with them.

Ted arrived at the front and saw that the entry that Jerome and he had garnered a first prize award for the apple butter category. He was immediately filled with excitement, pride, and elation as he tried to scan the crowd behind him for Jerome. As he turned, he felt someone pulling his shoulder towards him and hoped it was Jerome. It was not. It was Janelle.

"Good job, little brother, I'm so proud of you!"

Ted hugged her back.

"Thank you! Grandma Ruthie would be proud."

As Janelle and Ted turned side by side, holding each other's shoulders, Greg Hillcrest started to walk up the steps of the stage to begin the ceremony. Ted stood up on his toes to scan the crowd and the back entrance to see if Jerome was in attendance. No Jerome

"Hi... hello... hello, can you hear me? Is this thing on?" Greg Hillcrest's voice sounded hoarse, and he looked haggard. His polo shirt was only tucked in on one side of his khakis, and his hair a bit disheveled. Like he had just woken up from a bender of some sort. "It is my great honor to start the awards ceremony for this year's Apple Butter Festival. As chairman and CEO of Hillcrest Orchards, I can say that we are thrilled and thankful for all the effort of both the citizens of Hubert and also you, the visitors to our town, who will experience the great wonder of what makes this place a great American town. I encourage everyone, before they leave today, to look at all our wonderful products that are now being distributed all over the world. It makes a big difference to the economy and people of this great town. Without further ado, I'll give the microphone to our coordinator of this year's awards, Mr. S!"

Greg Hillcrest immediately exited the stage and scuttled out of the awards tent in a hurry. Ted noticed his facial expression quickly change from pleasant to angry and emotionally disturbed. He brushed it off as he leaned into Janelle, still basking in having received the first place award.

Mr. S. Went through all the other winners of the awards and shook everyone's hands, including Ted's. Each awardee took a photo with Mr. S. that would be used for the catalog and PR for the promos for next year's festival. Ted received his award money, and noticed they'd also included two #1 ribbons - one for both him and Jerome. While standing on the stage, he was scanning to see if Jerome was there to join him. He was not, though he did smile when he saw Janelle doing the same money dance from breakfast earlier that day. Laughing, he stepped down off the stage and hugged her, "God, it sucks Jerome isn't here... I might walk over to the orchard to see if I can find him. "

"Sounds like a plan."

They both wandered off separate ways out of the awards tent. As Ted walked out of the festival gates and down the street towards the Hillcrest Orchards, he still felt something unsettling in the pit of his stomach. And it wasn't the seven pancakes he'd eaten. Something was definitely off. He just didn't know what it was. He also felt at a loss for words, let alone actions. Jerome and he were forbidden from socializing with or seeing each other, and he didn't want to get either of them in trouble by asking around too much. He walked past Hillcrest Estate and tried to see into Jerome's second story bedroom window. The shades were closed. Perhaps he was just sick? He walked down the aisles of the tree orchard past Aisle 6 Tree 7. The note he wrote Jerome the previous day was still there.

Ted spent the rest of the afternoon meandering all over

Nighttime Kingdom

town, walking behind the banners, gates, rides, lines, and shouts of families unabashedly enjoying their joyous weekend. They were all so blissfully unaware of what it was like to have to be powerless to survive. This numbness was something most rarely felt. This festival was constructed and created for them to hold hands. To touch. To exist in the ways that Ted craved and longed to express himself in with Jerome. But no, he had to walk in the shadows. Their collaborative entry into the contest was one of few ways to express their togetherness. They could not walk hand in hand, laughing together like the rest of the town could while gleefully enjoying their caramel apples. True, they could be brave and display their affections, but that would be foolish. The leering eyes would latch onto them even before any real affection was displayed. Boys don't walk this way together. But this was the only way he knew how to exist. It was all too subtle, this powerless dance he felt that morning while wandering around the town looking for Jerome. It was such an effort to appeal to his cause while remaining casual, feigning disinterest while asking about his whereabouts. Just keep it casual. Like checking in on a long-lost cousin that had no emotional attachment. Just bored and wanting to hang out with someone on the hayrides, or share a conversation during the pancake breakfast.

It all felt like an exhausting compromise, like a rock in the pit of his stomach that had expanded into a bowling ball. That weight stemmed from a fear of the truth of what was going on. What if someone found out? It was only a matter of time before a tap on the shoulder would come and he would be brought into a private room of some sort to be instructed or reprimanded for his natural desires. While other high schoolers were considering the best carnival ride to go on that Saturday afternoon, Ted was contemplating the worst-case scenarios concerning himself and Jerome. A sense of dread continued to fill his body and intermingled with a surge of anxiety. He decided to go home to lay down for the rest of the afternoon. He entered his room and got into his bed and curled himself into the fetal position around the apple butter jar that their love had filled, with the cash winnings and two ribbons beside him.

Something was wrong, but what could he do? Ted Sr. and Greg Hillcrest had made it clear they were forbidden to see one another. He couldn't talk to Greg Hillcrest, and for sure couldn't reach out to the head foreman, Mr. Wilson. Now it was a waiting game. Doing something—doing anything—would only make matters worse. The last option would be waiting to see Jerome on the first day of school. He would surface soon. Ted closed his eyes, still clutching the jar, and fell asleep.

Saturday dusk to dawn, **September 22nd, 1983**

Tap. Tap. Tip. Tap. It was hard to decipher between the rain and the sound of something hitting Ted's window. He arose from his slumber and sat up in his bed. *Tap. Tap.* He sat up and looked out the window. There was a figure outside, waving. He slowly whispered to the huddled mass, "I will let you in come to the front door,"

When Ted opened the front door, he saw only a shadowed figure with a hoodie start emerging towards the screen door. He gestured again, whispering, "Come in, nice to see you."

As the figure came through the screen door, Ted could recognize it was Jerome... but it was also not Jerome. He had a swollen eye, and was visibly limping while making his way across the threshold.

"I didn't have anywhere else to go. Hope it is okay I came here."

"Of course it is," Ted whispered, gesturing to Jerome to enter the kitchen and sit down by the table.

Nighttime Kingdom

"Don't worry, he is totally out, drunk as usual. and won't know anything that is going on," Ted got up and slowly closed the bedroom door, noticing Ted Sr. passed out on his bed. He also walked to Janelle's door and closed it before returning back to the kitchen. By that point, Jerome had lowered his hood and Ted could see more clearly the gruesome details of his face and head. He had visible cuts under both eyes, and deep bruising on his neck.

"Are you... okay? I was so worried. I was looking for you all of the Festival."

"I am okay... I..." Jerome sputtered out, coughing, with his hand visibly shaking to cover it before resting on the kitchen table. "Some bad things happened last night." Then he looked down and softly wept.

Ted got up, stood beside Jerome and cradled his head into his stomach. When Jerome raised his head a moment later, a stain of blood had transferred to Ted's t-shirt.

"Let's get you out of these wet and dirty clothes, and into a hot bath. I will put what you're wearing in the washer."

They quietly walked into the bathroom, on the other side of the kitchen, and closed the door. Ted helped Jerome take off his hoodie, as he was clearly struggling to navigate pulling his shoulders through. Jerome placed his hoodie on the ground and Ted saw his arms were also visibly bruised and cut. He gently placed his hand on his arm and whispered, "Who did this to you? I am going to kill them."

Jerome looked at himself in the mirror and said, "Well, isn't this lovely? How am I going to hide any of this now?"

"You don't need to worry about that. Let's get the rest of these clothes off," Ted sighed, as he turned on the water in the bath and checked the temperature. Then he turned towards Jerome, who was still shaking uncontrollably, and helped him remove his t-shirt. This revealed deep lacerations on his back. "We need to take you to a doctor. You look seriously hurt."

"No... I can't. It will only make matters worse. I am okay."

"Well you don't look like it."

Ted turned away and grabbed a towel for Jerome to stand on as he continued to undress and wad up the remaining dirty clothes to be washed. As Jerome took off his underwear, he noticed there were dried blood stains. Ted helped Jerome lower himself down into the tub. The water at that point was just an inch or so, and was still filling up. As Jerome settled into the tub, he would see the blood start coming off his body and blossoming into the clean water. It was a beautiful, disgusting, and terrifying sight. Ted got up and walked to the bathroom closet for a washcloth. When he returned, Jerome was sitting with his head between his legs and sobbing. He knelt next to the tub and placed a shaky hand on Jerome's back, gently massaged it, and said softly, "It is okay. It is going to be okay. We need to get you cleaned up and I am going to wrap some of these wounds with an herb and witch hazel wrap."

Jerome looked up from the bathwater and turned towards Ted, his eyes visibly swollen and filled with a mixture of tears and blood. The resulting pink-ish mixture was pouring down his face as he tried to mutter to Ted while struggling for breath. Ted leaned towards him and kissed his cheek, not saying anything.

"I am so sorry I didn't make it to the festival today. My father... h-h-he did not let me," he looked down again into the water, as Ted gently began washing his back. "This is so embarrassing. I'm so sorry I am here, burdening you like this."

"You are not burdening me. You do not need to apologize."

Jerome pulled Ted closer to him and gently whispered, "He has done terrible things to me my whole life. He thinks I am an animal he can train... I do not know what I am going to do."

Nighttime Kingdom

Ted transitioned to distract himself from the unfolding situation before him by walking again to the bathroom closet to grab some shampoo and conditioner, "For now, you just need to clean up and then we can make a plan for the next steps."

"He took me to the barn. He tied me up like an animal," Jerome sobbed. "He beat me like a fucking animal. He kept saying... over and over... 'I will train you into what it is to be a man. I will show you what and who a real man is'."

Ted just sat there quietly, listening next to the tub. He noticed his hand was shaking and he tried to conceal this anxiety from Jerome, who was now hunched over even more in the tub. He grabbed the washcloth that had fallen off Jerome's back and wrung it out. For a moment, they both sat together in silence, looking down motionless. Ted looked upwards and noticed the window in the bathroom had become filled with the moisture in the room. It was as if their tears had flooded the whole space, and the weather inside was nothing other than helpless damp sorrow.

"Ted... he did things to me, Ted. Bad things."

Ted looked down at Jerome, then got down on his knees and leaned towards him. "It is okay... it's... I am just glad you're here."

"Ted, don't worry, he doesn't know about us. The secret stuff. He was mad when he found out I was sneaking away in the orchards. Someone told him, I'm not sure who. And what set him off was seeing the apple butter entry we submitted today."

"I am so sorry. I never wanted this to happen."

"It's not because of you. It is him. He is a monster. I am not sure what I am going to do."

"Well, for now I know I am going to go and get you some fresh clothes to wear and put your stuff in the dryer, are you okay to be alone for a second?"

151

"I am as okay as I can possibly be in my current state," Jerome laughed, and raised his hands gesturing over his body.

Ted walked over to the tub and pulled the stopper from the bottom and the multicolored soapy mixture started to drain. Let's get you up now and shower everything off," Ted said softly, while doing his best to smile as he helped Jerome stand and then pulled the shower curtain closed as the shower came on.

"Okay, I will be back in a second. I'm going to make you some wraps for your back and your eyes with a recipe I learned from Ruthie."

Nighttime Kingdom

Ted exited, closing the bathroom door behind him softly before walking into the kitchen. Looking for the first available place to sit, he meandered to the nearest chair. When he landed, he started uncontrollably crying and shaking. He felt a strong panic and heat surging through his whole body, and a spell of dizziness made him place his head in his hands on the table. His breath was fast, shallow, and labored. *What monsters do these horrible things?* He could hear the water splashing in the bathroom from where he was sitting, and got up and opened the washer and started to place Jerome's clothes into the dryer. Scared, but also terrified, he looked down into Jerome's underwear. There were only slight unnoticeable stains removed, but the traces of the mud and blood stains from just an hour earlier had left a permanent impression. Why were people such monsters? What was this fear about anything that was different? Men are not born monsters. Monsters are formed at the hands of their fathers. These are not men who inflict such bruises. It was a true weakness to express such violence towards a helpless child. It was too much to digest, especially for a seventeen-year-old kid.

He walked into the spice pantry and pulled the spices he could recall from memory from the healing recipes he had observed from Grandma Ruthie. Witch hazel, for sure. Turmeric. Cinnamon. Warming spices. Spices that reduce inflammation, also. Remembering what the healing herbs for inflammation were, he grabbed chamomile. Comfrey. Yarrow. He pulled them together into a bowl and mixed them with some mustard oil and witch hazel before placing them in a cheesecloth satchel. Two separate packs, one for Jerome's eye and the other for his back. As he was exiting the spice pantry, he saw Jerome was standing in the kitchen and looking forlornly out the window.

"This storm is going to ruin the harvest this year. It is out of everyone's control. The reason why I couldn't see you over the weekend was because my family was entertaining investors from out of town that were looking to buy the company. My father says we are going bankrupt. It was the beginning of the buildup to last night. I will never forgive him for what he did to me, Ted. I feel trapped... like I have nowhere to go."

He turned towards Ted, and walked towards him and they embraced and Jerome started crying again.

"All we can do for now is survive. One day at a time. Keep our heads low until we have the power and the means to leave this town."

"But don't you see, Ted, I can't leave! There is nowhere for me to go. I am not as strong as you are. I am not sure... I don't know. I feel so scared. I feel trapped. I do not see a way out of this for me."

"There is always a way out. You just need to ask for help."

"Who am I going to ask for help? The person who would help fix the problem in this town is the monster causing it."

"You're right. What about your mom?"

"She is like a wet blanket. Totally frozen and paralyzed in her own fear of him also. I'm just so scared, Ted. I don't know what to do."

"Well, for now we need to focus on getting you fixed up. I put together a healing spice pack for your eyes and back. Let me get a change of clothes for you from my room first, before we apply these."

Jerome laid a quilt out on the table that'd been used for decades by Grandma Ruthie. He gave Jerome the clothes from his room and he put them on slowly, wincing from the pain. They both laughed when they looked at Jerome's appearance.

"Well... if the guys from football practice could see me now!"

Ted gestured for Jerome to get on the table, face down.

Nighttime Kingdom

He stood beside Jerome and briefly connected with his feet to the ground. Ted turned his head towards the sky and connected with the space between his hands, warming them before placing them gingerly on Jerome's back. He slowly applied the compress. He could see the open lacerations where a belt had left its bite, and in some places where its buckle had. *Why are people such monsters?* His hand trembled as he placed the first spice pack on Jerome's back. He could sense him recoil as he mindfully wrapped the cheesecloth around his stomach and back area twice, to ensure it was secure.

"I would just keep this on for the night. It will do wonders for the swelling, and by morning hopefully you can feel better about walking around in public. What will you say when people ask?"

"Like every good actress, I will say I fell," he laughed and then winced from the pain of doing so.

They both transitioned into Ted's room and sat on his bed. The pair were looking towards the floor with expressions that screamed shell shock and exhaustion; Ted's from witnessing the violence inflicted on Jerome, and Jerome's from the state of confusion, shock, and denial about what had occurred to him at the hands of his father. How can you possibly forgive someone who brought you into this world but is now actively trying to remove you from it? The mood in the room was quiet. As they both sat on the bed, Jerome draped his free arm around Ted and said, "I have no regrets about any of it, just so you know. But we won't be able to talk anymore after this, not for a long while."

"That makes me very sad. But I understand. Hopefully we can still talk at school. You know where to find me, in the library or art room."

"We'll definitely still talk. I appreciate our friendship... but after yesterday, well, I am afraid that you will get hurt and I do not want that to happen. I couldn't live with that."

"You do not need to worry about me," Ted turned, looking towards Jerome and meeting his eyes. It was hard to look at him in that state. The bath and the cleaning of the wounds had helped improve things, but the deeper wounds of the situation would take a long time to heal. It was a compromising dance for both of them to decide how much of their core selves they were willing to give up in the face of the intolerance of the town they both were resigned to live in for another year, until they turned eighteen.

"On a lighter note," Ted said, as he pulled out the jar of apple butter, the two ribbons and the cash envelope. "Can you believe we won first prize!? There is still hope in the world. You should keep half of the money, and here is your ribbon."

"This is so great! I don't think I have ever won anything, let alone #1."

There was a shaky tenderness that held them together as the rays of the moon danced through the curtain windows tickling their backs. Ted raised his hand, noticing the shadows had formed an image of a rabbit he portrayed just two weeks ago while they were laying on their backs and tracing their dreams onto one another's skin. Jerome looked up and raised his hand also, meeting Ted's, and they pretended to talk with the shadows. For just a moment, things were almost normal for them.

Ted gently touched Jerome's shoulder and got up off the bed to walk to the closet.

"I'm excited to show you something."

"I cannot deal with any more surprises tonight!"

"Don't worry, it will be a nice surprise."

Ted parted the row of hung shirts, dress pants, and work overalls, then started to crawl into the back cove space of the closet.

Nighttime Kingdom

"Hey, can you actually grab those pillows off the bed and the blankets"

Jerome handed them to Ted, and he pulled them inside before going further in and disappearing. A hand then emerged, beckoning to Jerome. He grabbed it and let it lead the way as he also crawled into the closet. Ted positioned the pillows in the back and they both laid down next to one another, gazing up towards the pointed ceiling that'd been decorated over the years with cutouts and drawings by Ted.

"This is one of my favorite places to go to when I need to feel safe."

"I love it. It is like a living, breathing world of Ted!"

As the pair laid down, they allowed the glimmering of the lights and the shapes and shadows to soothe them as their nervous systems finally began to settle.

"Thanks again, Ted. I truly appreciate everything you have done for me."

As the night wore on, so did the storm outside. You could hear the relentless pattering of the rain and pounding of the branches hitting the roof along the sides of the horse barn house. The wind howled so hard that its anger even reached the cavern of the closet cove where Jerome and Ted were laying, side by side. Their breath and hearts matched the ferocity of it. Shifting back and forth, side over side and back to back, they both fell into a fitful sleep. But that took some time. For a great while, Ted laid wide awake staring at the ceiling. Despite the wind, he could hear the delicate scampering of the mice.

A small crack of the place where the wooden beams were pushed and pulled from the wind. A subtle wrinkle and rustle of the pillow beside him where Jerome laid his head. How could he even begin to process the events of last night? Occasionally, Jerome would twitch in his sleep, moan, talk aloud, and at one point he even started punching the air. Ted gently pulled him closer, and slowly rocked him back and forth to awaken and then allowed him to return to a deep sleep, noticing the sound of his breathing shifting. They held each other close, and it was a closeness that was felt mutually. This was to be the last night they were likely to spend with one another, and so it burned all the more brightly. The quiet rise and fall of sleeping breath mixed with the tears of the rain on the window matched Ted's own heart. Each knew the contours of the other's body. It represented a familiarity, a map of both their hearts intertwined. It felt like they could have perhaps been on a boat inside the closet cove, swaying from side to side, switching and rotating arms and legs, on top and over and amidst one another to stay warm.

As Jerome and Ted laid together in the back cove of Ted's closet, you could see the shadows of the lightning and fingers and toes of the branches tapping on the window. The events of the previous day and night had shocked them both. The warmth of their bodies was still apparent beneath the darkness each of them was navigating. Ted still felt a warmth and a light, even within the oppressive darkness that was descending all around him. The deepest recesses of the heart are always present, even at the darkest hours of night.

While Ted slept that night, he had a dream in which three angels came down from the sky and surrounded both Jerome and him while they slept. The light of their hands underneath them overpowered everything and they ascended with both Ted and him towards the clouds. They circled around both, and there was a warm, embracing presence that engulfed them. He touched one of the angel's palms and could feel the warmth of their hand that raced through his own and up his arm and into his chest. It formed a circular pattern that resembled the galaxy formations that Jerome had pointed out while they were

Nighttime Kingdom

laying watching the night sky the summer before. He looked towards Jerome, and saw that they had the same galaxy patterns across their chests. As he reached forward to touch Jerome's chest, he felt a shaking hand reaching to wake him.

"I need to get going, before anyone knows I was here. I have to get back home."

They both crawled out of the cove and started getting dressed.

"Let me get your clean clothes out of the dryer, one second."

Ted quickly exited the room and retrieved Ted's clothes from the dryer. He looked into the garbage and saw the filthy rags that he had used the previous night to clean Jerome's wounds. The sight of them sent a quiver through his spine and into his stomach and heart. He quickly removed the garbage bag and returned to his bedroom, giving Jerome his clothing. As Jerome dressed, Ted looked out his bedroom window and noticed there was a blanket of frost that had enveloped all of the tree branches outside from the storm.

"No one is going to be happy about this early frost, especially the apples."

"You can say that again. I am looking forward to this entire harvest season being over."

Ted helped Jerome get back into his hoodie and remove the bandage that was covering his eye. The swelling had decreased significantly, and he could see out of that eye again, but a rainbow of purple, yellow, and red splotches had formed that extended all the way up his forehead.

"Well... the good news is that you can see you have an eye again, the bad news is you look pretty... uhhh... weathered."

"This is where I am at. I am afraid to go back home, but I have to face the music."

"Just know you can always come back here if you need to,"

Ted said with as much confidence as he could muster, placing his hand on Jerome's shoulder as they both quietly exited the house and stepped out onto the frost-kissed sidewalk.

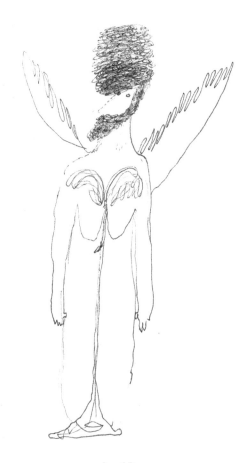

Angel Protector

The ice storm from the night before had frozen all the trees and their branches, changing the leaves overnight. It was as if the entire town of Hubert were encased in a time capsule of that last night. As they both started walking along Middleton Road, towards Jerome's house, their shoes crunched silently.

Nighttime Kingdom

Ted turned to Jerome and limped on one foot and then drew another line with his other foot, "So it looks like a vampire came and stole the other person in the middle of the night."

Ted glanced over at Jerome as a sigh of relief washed over him. He was okay. But there was also a sense of impending terror about what lay ahead in their future. Their sneakers were the only footprints on the sidewalk for a moment. Oranges, reds, and spots of blue surfaced as delicate patterns of light reflected off the bark of each tree as the sun began to rise on Middleton Road.

All Ted wanted to feel was to feel safe with Jerome. But when you have no parachute to catch you, a lingering feeling of not being able to let your guard down will endure. You can't afford to fall. The burden of himself and everything he needed or desired laid solely and squarely on his own shoulders. That weight never fades. It stalks you, haunts you, and weighs you down with the shackles of living in a body or identity that is just not you. Your heart and soul grow weary. There is no choice for these beautiful souls, who exist outside the constraints of the society that they were born into. You just so happen to wake one day—oftentimes by accident, perhaps even under an apple tree—with the jock from school you never talked to. When you awaken to your true nature, you can either cut the ties that bind you or suffer in silence.

Neither option comes for free. The pain of hiding your true self from the world is sometimes a temporary salve for a larger, gaping wound inside. It was clear Ted and Jerome were at different points along the timelines of their awakenings. Ted was already an outcast. Jerome was not. Both remained unsure of who they were as boys, and did not know yet who they were as men. But one thing was clear. Ted knew the tenderness he felt in his heart toward Jerome. It was an awakening that was too bright, too painful to ignore. Inwardly, he would vow to never surrender to the rules and constraints placed on him by societal forces and past generations. He knew there was just a year left. And when he could leave, and fly away from Hubert, he would find a home that was for him and that was more him. Walking down the sidewalk next to Jerome, with his limp and busted eye, he knew one thing - every moment looking into Jerome's eyes was a reflection of what felt right inside. He would never deny himself the right to feel love and have another person love him back. It just so happened that other person was another boy, and a boy just as confused as he was by figuring out what it meant for him to become a man.

Jerome stopped Ted, beneath a sycamore tree that still had a dusting of ice on it that was starting to melt and merge back into the bark.

"It's weird... this bark almost looks like a map of Ohio, doesn't it? Maybe one day we will be able to create our own map. On our own street. In a town where we can be ourselves."

"Yeah, maybe someday."

"Do you think the Festival is still going to happen today?"

"Probably, this town has no other choice."

"Will I see you later, at the festival hopefully?

"That sounds nice, but I am still grounded... so probably won't be seeing you until the first day of school, on Monday."

Ted shoved Jerome jokingly goodbye as they usually did to show their affection publicly, and they both turned and walked in separate directions. Ted did so on only one foot, in a hopping motion, "So everyone thinks a vampire was here, not a human."

Monday, September 24th, 1983

Save us our souls from harm and lead us on our way
Save us from suffering when we are lead astray

Nighttime Kingdom

Protect us as we lay down to rest for the day

That Monday morning, Jerome Hillcrest was found hanging from a tree in the Hillcrest family orchard. Frankie Wilson, the son of head foreman Ted Wilson, found him while out walking the dog. It was Aisle 2, Row 6, Tree 7. He was still wearing the same clothes from the previous night. He had pinned a button of the Hubert town motto from the Apple Butter Festival to his chest, as well as the #1 blue ribbon that Ted had given him the night before.

The Hillcrest family did not report his death publicly, and there was no memorial, funeral, or public obituary.

During his senior year after Jerome died, Ted wrote the following letters that are currently in Rita's baby book:

November 7th, 1983

JJ,

Feels weird to write you here, after everything that happened, but Mr. S. was talking to us in class today about trying to write letters to loved ones as a way to practice for writing cover letters for our home economics class and I thought at first I was going to write a letter to Grandma Ruthie, but thought I would try with you since he said it should be someone that you definitely loved unconditionally.

Mr. S. has been pretty nice to me actually, after everything that happened with you. It was really weird at first, and I felt like I couldn't go to the library or drugstore without people staring at me, but after a while things quieted down and everyone returned to their own dramas. It was definitely weird to start the first day of school without you being there.

William J. O'Brien

If it makes you feel any better, the football team this season has done terribly! I really feel it is because you are missing and they do not know how to move on without you. Some of those guys actually have said hi to me in the halls, but that is about it. I keep to myself and that is just fine with me.

I found out about what happened in the most awful way. My dad got into a really big fight. I said some harsh words to him, but you would have been proud of me since the second time he tried to hit me I grabbed his hand and let him know what I thought. After that, he has pretty much left me alone which has been nice.

It has been really hard to not see you. I was beyond upset about how they did not have any memorial or funeral for you. It was if they'd just erased you from the planet. Like you never existed. Your mom and dad quickly afterwards left town and were nowhere to be found. Even to this day, the gravestone where you are buried just has your name and date of birth, but no date listed for your death. I know you're buried there, since I saw the dirt a few weeks afterwards from the road. No one in town talks about it, probably because everyone is scared of losing their jobs. I know they sold the company to a big Japanese corporation. My dad has been happier though, since he was promoted to corporate as a result. What a world we live in! Who knew that apparently there is a big demand for American apple products abroad?

Well anyway, I miss you terribly. Mr. S. keeps talking to me about what I am going to do. All I know is that I am leaving this town the day school is over and I turn eighteen and I am not looking back.

Nighttime Kingdom

The last thing I wanted to say is that I still have your shirt from that night, which is embarrassing. I sleep with it under my pillow every night. Thanks for looking out for me.

T

June 12th, 1984

JJ,

Well, believe it or not, tomorrow is graduation day from Hubert High School! I do not have very much to report, except that I am writing to let you know I survived senior year of high school. It was pretty uneventful for the most part... except around the end of winter break, when Janelle dyed my hair pitch black so it was fun to play the role of a vampire around town. Tomorrow I am planning on leaving Hubert and getting on a bus to NYC. It seems really scary, but I am proud of myself for leaving and feel like I want to write something so you know I am actually getting out like we always talked about. I sometimes visit the tree—our tree—in the orchard at night. The company is now owned by a different person, and they are not as strict as before. Mrs. Wilson, the foreman's wife, has also been really nice to me. I am sure you know already that she is the head librarian, and after what happened she always let me stay in the library for as long as I wanted, even outside the designated time and she lets me use the computers as much as I want and order any weird books to transfer to check out. It seems weird to leave my cove, but I decided the only things I am taking to NYC with me, besides the essentials, will be Rita's baby book and your shirt. I still

165

have it, but at this point it is pretty worn down from all of my tears and drool from my pillow! Anyways, wish you were coming with me.

Love you ,
T

Chapter 13
Return

The morning light scratched at Ted's eyes as he sat on the tarmac at LaGuardia, preparing to take off for his flight to begin his long day to and from Cleveland Hopkins. It was a relatively short journey, but the two different places felt worlds apart. As the captain came on the intercom to inform the passengers that they were next to take off, he tried to rest and placed the back of his head on the pillow rest behind him.

It was always hard with the naked eye to comprehend the enormity of the city, but during these times it almost seemed feasible. All the buildings were really just little boxes that had windows of different shapes and sizes. And they all coexisted so peacefully. Or, at least it seemed that way in the brief silence of 6 am. The plane transitioned to the runaway and had a small pass before the speed and sound gradually increased and they took off. Why was returning and going home just as painful as his return to NYC? He felt a sense of relief as he looked down towards his stowaway bag in front of him to make sure he'd brought all the keys and paperwork necessary for the closing of the sale of the ole' Krieger barn house that still sat so cozy off the main square of Hubert. Ever since Ted Krieger passed away, there really was no use in holding onto it. Janelle now lived in the suburbs of Chicago, and was delightfully content with her husband and three children. She shared similar but different scars from their childhood in Hubert, and did not return very often either. They both came back whenever Ted Sr. was actively sick and needed extra support, and both were there at his bedside when he died. He remained a bachelor to the very end. The decor inside the horse barn had changed since Ted and Janelle left. Now it was mostly lined with car posters and the remnants of items left over the years from various members of the Krieger family.

Shortly after he left for NYC, in an ironic twist of fate, Ted's room was transformed into a weight room for his father to work out in. By the time Ted has departed, all traces of his secret cove in the back of his closet were removed, except a few traces of his dreams in the form of sticker residue that stubbornly clung to the walls and ceilings.

As the plane gained altitude and leveled, the seatbelt sign was turned off and the quick beverage service circulated. He'd made his trips to Hubert progressively shorter over the years, and some like today would be an all in one trip. The memories and familiarity of the past seemed too much for Ted's psyche if he remained in town for more than 48 hours. As the stewardess gave Ted his coffee, the elderly woman knitting next to him said, "Always need my coffee too in the morning, do not know who I would be without it!" Ted slightly laughed as he stirred cream into his cup and watched it swirl.

"Business or pleasure?"

"A little bit of both. Taking care of closing on my family's house, then tying up some loose ends in town before I head back later tonight."

Nighttime Kingdom

"Yes, these transitions are always humbling. May I ask where you grew up?"

"Hubert. Not a lot of people know where it is at. But it is a small town, just south and a little bit east of Cleveland. My science teacher always said that if you folded Lake Erie in half and moved your finger down slowly, you'd find Hubert smack dab in the middle, between Cleveland and Middleton. Not sure if that is totally accurate, but it sure makes for a good story."

"Yes, I love it! Of course I know Hubert. My family would every year travel to the Apple Butter Festival. What a beautiful town. You must feel so lucky to have grown up in such a pastoral place as that!"

Ted couldn't bring himself to disagree. He just nodded and smiled and they both silently settled back into their seats and the plane landed into Cleveland. Ted picked up the rental car and started driving towards Hubert. The main highways and more concentrated areas of buildings and towns and strip malls slowly gave way to two lane highways, then single lane roads and dots of farms.

Hubert was at the top of a hill. That was the last part, and the part that felt like the hardest for Ted. It was a symbol of going back up to the place he always wanted to leave. He parked his car in the front driveway of the horse barn and went inside. All the rooms were empty, only a few scraps of paper remained that he started to clean up with a garbage bag. He went to the back door and stepped outside to see the fire ring was still there. He looked towards the tree and saw the Cardinal's nest was still there, but there were no occupants today.

"Hello? Anyone home?"

"Out here! Just cleaning out some items!"

Ted walked into the kitchen and was met by the realtor and the new couple who were buying the property. Another hilarious twist of fate was that this would be their second home. They wanted somewhere to go to de-stress from the city, and after going to the Apple Butter Festival last September had fallen in love with the town and decided it would fit the bill.

"Nice to finally meet you. This house has been in my family for over a hundred years. There have been many memories and stories created here, especially in this kitchen, thanks to Grandma Ruthie."

They proceeded to finalize the paperwork for the transfer of sale and Ted handed them the keys. As he was about to step out the front door for the last time, he paused "Can I do one last walk around?" He went into his bedroom then, and opened the closet door and climbed inside the back cover and was barely able to lay down. It was hard to believe that two battered young men had once slept in this space for a night. Getting out, he placed his hand on the carving that read 'Jerome and Ted' on the wooden beam, then left without saying goodbye to the new owners. Though he didn't drive away. He got his bag out of the rental car and started walking towards the old Hillcrest Estate and Cannery. About a year after Jerome died, the big corporation it was sold to turned the main house into a spa and bed and breakfast. It was all open to the public now, and they gave hayrides and tours to groups to teach them about apple growing and how to make cider, applesauce, and the various apple products that were still being distributed worldwide.

The Hillcrest Family Cemetery remained intact, though, and stood as it always had just behind the gardens and across the street from the public cemetery. Ted first walked to the Krieger family plots where Karl, Grandmother and Grandfather Krieger, and now his own father was buried. He placed a packet of apple seeds on Karl's grave, a packet of cigarettes on Grandpa Krieger's, a spice satchel he'd made on Ruthie's, and a fifth of vodka on his father's. After ceremoniously placing the items, he stepped back and felt the breath on his cheeks and neck. Ruthie was saying hi and giving him a kiss, "I love you, my little man."

He transitioned over to the Hillcrest family cemetery next, to Jerome's grave. The headstone just said 'Jerome Hillcrest.' Ted placed a jar of apple butter, with a blue ribbon, on Jerome's grave and stepped back before murmuring, "Love you, wish you were here, and I miss you so much. I made apple butter yesterday for my best friend Shantel's engagement party. Anyways, I really wish you were here, but I now understand why you couldn't stay. It was too much."

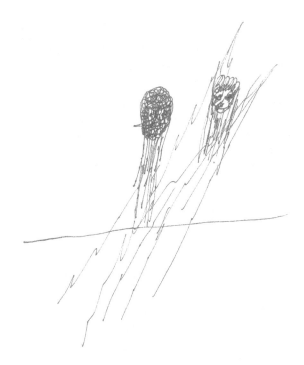

As he put his hand over Jerome's carved name, two birds—a cardinal and blue jay—landed on the graves on either side of him. They stopped, tweeted and sang, and then flew into the orchard. Ted smiled and wiped his tears and walked back to the car and drove back to the airport in silence, but not before placing one last thing on his first love's grave. It was the last letter young Ted wrote to Jerome, which was never given to him.

September 24th, 1983

JJ,

I woke up this morning and still could not believe that you are gone. I am not sure how I will be able to move forward in this life and this world without knowing and having your presence next to me. I feel like my heart is torn open and bleeding and there are not enough words in all of the languages put together to write what I am supposed to say. So I'll just say it plainly. You meant more to me than anyone else ever has. I wish I would have told you how I really felt, but I was just too scared. I bitterly wish I could have protected you from the terror of your father. I wish I was strong enough to be able to protect both of us. I wish I was so many things. I now only wish you are at peace. I did not know you were suffering so much and were in such agony. I am sorry that you did not feel like you had a way out. The last night we spent together was one of the most magical I can remember. You are my heart, and will forever be with me. Just know that I truly loved you, and I am sorry I never said or told you as much. I just was so scared. I will always remember your laugh. I will always remember the nights we spent in the orchards. I promise I will get out of this town, but I also feel like you should be with me to do it. I must admit to feeling mad that you did not come to me when you felt like you had no other choice. I am

Nighttime Kingdom

mad about what your father did to you your whole life, and especially that night in the barn. Know you are one of the most handsome, wonderful people in the world. I am not sure if I will ever love anyone as I have loved you. You were, and will forever be, the bedrock of my heart and soul.

With all my heart, broken and shattered,

T

Chapter 14
Home

Ted got off the F train. His stop. This stop. For now, this was his current destination. Home. While walking towards St. James Place, Ted was existing in the still, intermediate time when night and day remain apart but are flirting with each other before letting go until their next tryst. A subtle quiet surrounds this time in the city. It was one of his favorite times for that reason. Only the rats, club-goers, and one-night standers slithering through the darkness and shadows of the night to their resting places exist within it. The lights on the lamps, and the neon of the signs always seemed to have a fog hanging around them. It was like looking through a window that needs to be defrosted in the depths of winter. It was time to go to bed.

Rounding the corner of St. James Place, he noticed lights in an unusual number of homes were on still. Perhaps forgotten? Still awake? Restless and waiting for someone to return? A symbol for those lost that they could return to that home at some point. What was home, anyway? Where could it exist, and for how long? But for now, this was his home. He knew that something had shifted, if only for a minute, or second. A

Nighttime Kingdom

glimpse of the spaces usually by surprise we all find in-between errands, obligations, the momentum, and movement of the planet.

He looked up to the sky before the brownstone that Sam and he lived in. It was his home. Even if it always felt like a dream. Or a memory. Or even a potential. For now, it was his place. Where he was meant to be. He saw a star glimmer and thought to himself it was Jerome, or maybe his father? Or Grandma or Grandpa Krieger? Perhaps they were winking, as if to say, 'We are here. Do not let go or give up. It is not your time to leave.'

Ted knew in his heart that the bad things that'd transpired that weekend in Hubert had befallen him for a reason. Just as some of the self-help books he read stated "Traumas we experience are willed, magnetized by our subconscious, as an auspicious vehicle to create necessary forgiveness and healing inside of us." A wound festers under the surface until it receives the required resolution. These things reach a tipping point, at which they are no longer content remaining beneath the surface and being suppressed through distractions, addictions, and neurosis. Monsters and tragedies just don't appear. We will them into being, as spiritual crises, for radical change and healing. Or not. Maybe shit just happens. Maybe there is no silver lining.

In Ted's own experience, sometimes things are just that bad. That was the truth. There was no overarching and all-encompassing philosophical answer to all of it. It is what it was. And, through the moments of reprieve or insights, what these events yield is a regaining of what really matters deep down at our very core. The big questions of why we are here. Why we are alive.

To be at the bottom of the barrel and somehow resurface, to have the ability to genuinely be there for others when they experience these events, tragedies, and unexpected circumstances of what we are born into is perhaps the meaning of that shit. In the end, the meeting of whoever, however, and whatever you are is enough. At that intersection is what many people call 'heart.' It is life. It is meaning. Even if only for a split second. A glimmer of a connection. An edge. If it tastes bitter or sweet, or bittersweet, or sorrowful. Just being willing to taste life is enough.

The heroines are those who are willing to taste all the flavors and not hold their nose. Those who step boldly into the depths of the dumpster fire and open their every sense and pore to all of it. The only regrets that Ted will ever have again are not heeding this sentiment; not tasting life, but hiding in the shadows for fear of what could happen. What did happen. What did not happen. Who remembered what. Who blamed who. Who took on the loss and claimed it as their own. Who disregarded their role and blamed others for their cowardice.

There are minor losses. And losses that are life changing. Both are similar in the reactions they trigger in the spirit, heart, and soul. Then there are those losses which reverberate so deeply that they forever reshape the fundamental structure of who we are. Such losses are often tinged with nostalgia, since there is a desire to want to return to who that person was before or for things to go back to how they were before—and ignorance is bliss type of deal—but the most painful aspect of that is facing up to the fact of its impossibility. The fundamental structure of how you were built has changed. Kind of like when you accidentally break your favorite cup or bowl. You certainly can make every effort to repair and make it whole again, but will always, in every case, be some fragment you cannot locate or a crack that does not set correctly. You cannot become whole again. You can come to regard these imperfections as the gold. They can remind you of what you

Nighttime Kingdom

have lost, or of what you have been through gone through and emerged victorious from. You may use them to touch base with the motley crew of self-loathing, shame, and disgust inside yourself, but also have it mixed with the perfect beauty of the new you.

As always, our obsession with the phoenix rising from the ashes for a good triumphant ending to a tragic story must spread its wings. Oftentimes, when someone experiences trauma it can feel like many things. Among these is awkward. So, what you do is you stop talking about it. And you quietly go about your life, pretending on some level that you are now healed, and you do so more for the benefit of those around you. You end up reading books on self-improvement, and some will even say that you subconsciously willed these terrible things to happen as a vehicle to heal from something. Can you imagine? But there exists some truth there.

Ted could admit and see this for himself, after the events of September 20th, 1983 transpired. In the end, what it gave him was the courage to leave Hubert. Though he did not run away from it. He walked, tall and proud and slow and strong. In his heart, he carried and listened to what Jerome had said to him the night before he died, as they laid together for the last time.

"Promise, no matter what happens between us, that you will leave Hubert and live the life that we could never live here.

"I promise," Ted responded, and pulled Jerome in so tightly it was as if every one of their cells had become oppositely polarized magnets.

He knew that he made peace with himself. He knew that the innocence and life he had shared with Jerome were pure. Natural. Real. And, through all the searching he did in his adult life, he was finally able to see his true value. *He was a good person.* He was deserving of love. He was allowed to have sex with someone of any gender and be fully present, not a shell of a person. To allow his heart to be there. To allow his soul to breathe.

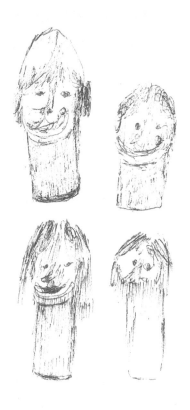

He ascended the stairs and entered the bedroom he shared with Sam. He was fast asleep. On the dresser sat photos of their relatives. When he was away in Hubert, Sam had enlarged a photo of Jerome from the scrapbook and framed it beside the rest of the family photos. Ted picked up the photo of Jerome, held it to his chest, and then placed it back on the nightstand and got into bed with Sam. He could feel his warmth like never before. He was there, present with him. It was a gift to be able to feel so close to another human body. Both hearts beating in

Nighttime Kingdom

sync together. He was here. On Earth. In Brooklyn, in this brownstone, with his lover. It was not a dream. He finally knew, without a shadow of a doubt, that he had done all he could. That was enough. Sam grabbed Ted's hand, pulling it around his chest and heart, "Love you baby, missed you, try to get some rest." Ted leaned into Sam's neck and kissed him and turned off the light.

Grand Krieger's Apple Butter recipe
(as translated by Ted Krieger)

At dawn, on the day closest to the new moon, at the end of the harvest season, when the air is moving from hot to warm, and the dew is still fresh, enter the fields. In the darkness, pick 7-8 apronfuls of apples. Choose apples that are multi-patterned, with a red and yellow surface, as if water from the night sky has kissed them with dew and left a birthmark.

Place the apples in shade for the rest of the morning. Wash the apples at noon, in fresh water. Dry them in the warm sun, under a family quilt of a loved one.

While the apples are drying, prepare the cooking place. Over a fire pit is best, burning wood that has been foraged from the same ground as the trees. Arrange a kindling pattern with the smallest sticks.

The cauldron or pot should be large enough to hold a great deal of liquid. Black is best for the pot. When the sun starts setting, light the fire. Place the finest apple cider in the barrel, at a quantity equal to the height of three apples. When the fire is starting to warm, then boil, core, peel, and quarter the apples.

Use a knife that has only been used for cooking fruit or vegetables or meat. Place the apples in the cauldron, and bring to a boil.

Apple Butter Recipe

Stir with a long wooden paddle. Never metal. Sit beside the fire with the people who are closest to your heart, and tell stories. Stir the apple butter periodically.

When the light of dawn starts to tickle the sky, add all your spices. Some use a special spice satchel bag made with cheesecloth. Reserve a small amount for two offerings.

Hold hands with your loved ones by the fire, and toss in the spices. The more natural spices the better. Cinnamon, nutmeg, cloves.

Then make an offering, to the right side of the cauldron, using your right hand for the land spirits. Then make an offering to the left side of the cauldron to those who have passed. Throw the rest towards the night sky.

At the first glimmer of the light of dawn, fill your jars.

Enjoy in the company of loved ones by the fireside on dark winter nights.

Acknowledgments

It goes without saying that no work of art happens in a vacuum. Art is always about the relationships that are involved in its creation, the conversations it sparks, and the connections it forms along the way. I am most grateful for Ed Jaeky, who has been a constant support throughout this process of both writing and releasing the book. I am also thankful to my siblings and close friends, especially Heather Kalamirades, Elizabeth Cross, John O'Brien, and Josh Faught, who were willing to read the first draft and offered constructive feedback and encouragement. The production and editing of this book would have never happened without the support of Callum, my copywriter and proofreader, and Ben Driggs, who offered precise secondary edits throughout the process. Additional thanks to John Schmid, who has been a longstanding supporter of both my artwork and experimentation within my practice. Additionally, I am grateful to all the artists and members of the Chicago art community. In the last chapters of this project, my students at the School of the Art Institute of Chicago continually offered inspiration and encouragement to pursue and advocate for claiming space for myself in the release of this project. Grateful to T. Cole Rachel and Ben Tousley for their support and encouragement for both the foreword and cover design. Lastly, I am grateful to my teachers, friends, family, and everyone from Northeast Ohio especially those who saw me and encouraged me to blossom into the confident queer adult I am today.

Resources

National Suicide Prevention Lifeline: 1-800-273-TALK (8255) - A free, confidential 24/7 helpline for individuals in crisis or emotional distress, providing support, information, and local resources.

Crisis Text Line: Text HOME to 741741 - A free, confidential text-based crisis intervention service available 24/7 for individuals in crisis, providing support and connecting them with trained crisis counselors.

The Trevor Project: 1-866-488-7386 - A leading national organization providing crisis intervention and suicide prevention services to LGBTQ+ youth, including a 24/7 confidential hotline, chat, and text support.

Substance Abuse and Mental Health Services Administration (SAMHSA): 1-800-662-HELP (4357) - A confidential and free helpline offering information, referrals,

Resources

and support for individuals and families facing substance use disorders and mental health challenges.

National Alliance on Mental Illness (NAMI) Helpline: 1-800-950-NAMI (6264) - A nationwide resource providing support, information, and referrals to individuals and families affected by mental illness, including depression, anxiety, PTSD, and more.

LGBTQ+ Community Centers: Local LGBTQ+ community centers often offer a range of support services, including counseling, support groups, and social events. Visit www.lgbtcenters.org to find a center near you.

Therapy and Counseling Services: Consider seeking support from a licensed therapist or counselor who specializes in trauma, LGBTQ+ issues, and mental health. Websites such as Psychology Today (www.psychologytoday.com) and Good-Therapy (www.goodtherapy.org) can help you find qualified professionals in your area.

Books and Resources: Explore literature and resources on trauma recovery, LGBTQ+ identity, and mental health. Some recommended books include "The Body Keeps the Score" by Bessel van der Kolk, "The Velvet Rage" by Alan Downs, and "Queer Voices: Poetry, Prose, and Pride" edited by Andrea Jenkins and John Medeiros.

Contributors

William J. O'Brien is an artist, writer, and educator based in Chicago. O'Brien's works are featured in collections worldwide, including those at the Cleveland Clinic, Miami Art Museum, and The Art Institute of Chicago. Originally from Northeast Ohio, as a child, he was part of the St. Helen's Unicycle Drill Team. Additionally, he is a professor of Ceramics at the School of the Art Institute of Chicago. *Nighttime Kingdom* is his debut novel.

T. Cole Rachel is a writer, editor, and teacher who lives in Brooklyn. His books include *Surviving the Moment of Impact* and *Bend, Don't Shatter*. He currently works as an editorial director at the New York Times.

Ben Tousley is a designer located in Marseille, France. He has been practicing design for seventeen years with a focus on music, editorial & branding projects.

Printed in the USA
CPSIA information can be obtained
at www.ICGtesting.com
LVHW062348130424
777255LV00009B/34